WHAT WOULD YOU SAY
IF YOUR BEST—AND ONLY—FRIEND
TOLD YOU HE WAS FROM MARS?

Well, that's just what Alan Mendelsohn told Leonard Neeble. And suddenly, it didn't matter if Leonard was chubby, wore glasses and wrinkly clothes and wasn't liked by anyone else at Bat Masterson Junior High in the snobby suburb of West Kangaroo Park.

What did matter were the plans Leonard and Alan made with their strange new friends at the Bermuda Triangle Chili Parlor. And before you could spell C3PO backwards, Leonard and Alan could make people and things do whatever they wanted them to! Imagine levitating your whole school. . . .

Bantam Books of related interest
Ask your bookseller for the books you have missed

Alan Mendelsohn, The Boy From Mars

Daniel M. Pinkwater

BANTAM BOOKS
TORONTO · NEW YORK · LONDON · SYDNEY

RL 6, IL 11 and up

ALAN MENDELSOHN, THE BOY FROM MARS

*A Bantam Book / published by arrangement with
Elsevier-Dutton Publishing Co., Inc.*

PRINTING HISTORY
E. P. Dutton edition published May 1979
2 printings through May 1980
Bantam edition / May 1981
2nd printing . . . September 1983

ISBN 0-553-24070-6

Published simultaneously in the United States and Canada

PRINTED IN THE UNITED STATES OF AMERICA

O   11 10 9 8 7 6 5 4 3 2

For Jill Miriam,
my Martian sweetie

TO CHRIS

Daniel Pinn

1

I got off to a bad start at Bat Masterson Junior High School. My family had moved from my old school district during the summer, and I didn't know a single kid at the school. On top of that, it turned out that kids at Bat Masterson put a lot of emphasis on how you look. This created a problem—I am a short, portly kid, and I wear glasses. Every other kid in the school was tall, had a suntan, and none of them wore glasses. Also clothes wrinkle up on me. I don't know why this should be—five minutes after I get dressed in the morning, everything is wrinkled. It looks like I slept in my clothes.

Not only did I not know anybody on my first day, not only did I find out that a short, portly, wrinkled kid with glasses is an outcast in that school, but I also sat down on somebody's half-finished Good Humor bar in the school yard. That reduced my confidence. Then it turned out that the school was not expecting me. My records, and grades, and whatever the old school was supposed to send, they had not sent—or they had sent them to the wrong place—or they had gotten lost.

So I had to sit on this bench in the office for most of the morning, sort of sticking to the bench because of the leftover Good Humor on the seat of my pants. Finally they gave me this big pile of cards to fill out. Then I had to run all over the school getting teachers to sign the cards. Three or four times I had to go back to the office with notes from teachers saying that their class was full, or it was the wrong class, or it conflicted with another class I was supposed to take.

And each time I entered a classroom, the class would giggle at me. Then the teacher would ask my name. It was written right at the top of every one of the cards—but the teacher would ask me to say it anyway. "Leonard Neeble," I would say, and the kids in the class would just go wild. I don't know why, but my name gets them every time.

At lunchtime I walked around the school yard. All the kids looked sort of grown-up and unwrinkled. Some of the girls even had lipstick on. The kids stood around in groups, talking and laughing. Some guys were showing off, walking on top of benches, and chasing each other, and hollering. Nobody looked at me or said anything to me. I had the feeling that if I tried to talk to anybody, they wouldn't have been able to hear me. I looked for a quiet spot to eat my tuna fish sandwich.

After lunch I went back to the office. The lady there had told me to come back at the beginning of each period. She looked at my cards and told me to go to gym class. I went. When I got to the gym, there was a bunch of kids sitting in rows on the floor. The teacher was standing on a bench. He was wearing su   and had a whistle on a lanyard around his neck. He had white sneakers on. I went around the kids sitting on the floor and came up to him from the side, holding out the card he was supposed to sign. "You're late, boy!" he said. He had a very loud voice.

"The lady in the office . . . I'm supposed to . . . this card . . . you have to sign my . . ." The teacher cut me off.

"Nobody comes late to gym!" he shouted. He really scared me. I could see all his teeth. "Anybody comes late to gym, he does five laps! Now do five laps, chubby—work off some of that lard. And while you're running, listen to what I'm telling the class."

I started running, holding my stack of cards.

"You will get two pairs of gym shorts, green; two pairs of sweat socks, white; you will get a sweat shirt, gray." The gym teacher was shouting at the class. His name was Mr. Jerris. His voice was so loud it made my ears hurt, even when I was making my turn at the far end of the gym.

"That's five, fat boy; take a rest," Mr. Jerris said. "Now, since none of you have any equipment, you can spend the rest of the period horsing around, QUIETLY!" Mr. Jerris spun around, jumped off the bench, and walked through a little door at the back of the gym.

I was sweating and out of breath. I expected the other kids to start up with "fat boy" and "chubby," after Mr. Jerris had called me those things—which was unfair, since I am actually not fat but portly. That's what it says on the label when I get clothes in the department store: boy's portly. The other kids didn't tease me. They didn't pay any attention to me at all. They went right to work, fooling with the gym equipment, doing handstands, swinging from the rings, and stuff like that. I looked at the door Mr. Jerris had gone through. I wondered if I should go and knock on it. I just stood there, holding my cards, for a long time.

Mr. Jerris came back. "I said QUIETLY!" His voice made an echo. "Come here, fatty, I'll sign that." I started to walk toward him. "RUN!" I ran. Mr. Jerris signed my card. "Now, by tomorrow, make sure you have at least gym shoes. By the end of the week, I want you to have all your equipment, got that . . ."—he looked at my card—"Neeble?" Mr. Jerris went back through the little door.

The gym class was the high point of the day for sheer unpleasantness, but all the other classes I went to were more or less the same—the teachers seemed annoyed that I was there, making them sign one more thing or send for an extra textbook—and not one kid said anything to me, although quite a few giggled at my name. By the time school let out and I started walking home, I was totally miserable.

Our new house was almost a mile from school, and I didn't like it. There wasn't one kid my age in the neighborhood. Except for some very little kids, babies really, a couple of blocks away, there were no kids at all. About the only good thing that had happened since we moved out of our old apartment in the old neighborhood was that my parents let me have a dog. The dog's name was Melvin, a big brown dog we got at the pound. I had had him since the middle of the summer, and he hadn't been able to learn a single trick. I spent about two weeks trying to teach Melvin to fetch a ball. I couldn't even get him to look at it. About the only thing Melvin could do that was sort of unusual was walk in his sleep. Still, he seemed to like me, and would take naps in my room, snoring and mumbling while I read or worked on a model airplane.

When I got home, Melvin was sleeping in the front hall. He opened one eye to say hello, and then dozed off. My mother was in the kitchen, cooking liver for Melvin's supper. Cooked liver was all he would eat. I hate the smell of liver cooking. The whole house smelled of it.

Everything in the house was still sort of new. My parents had bought all new furniture when we moved. My mother had picked out a lot of stuff for my room so it would look like a picture she had seen in a magazine. I wasn't allowed to put any tacks in the walls because of the plaid wallpaper, which was very expensive, but just perfect for a boy's room—my mother said. So I couldn't put up any posters or pictures or anything. I flopped down on my bed, which had a plaid bedspread to match the wallpaper. "How do you like your new school?" my mother shouted from the kitchen. I told her it was fine— what else could I say?

Melvin wandered in with his eyes half-open, and sort of crashed down on his elbows next to my bed. In thirty seconds he was snoring. I closed my eyes and tried to pretend we were still living in the old apartment.

2

The old apartment was in a neighborhood where none of the houses had lawns, and backyards were either concrete or dirt. There were a lot of kids around, and you could get into a ball game or a conversation or trade comics, just by going outside. It didn't seem to matter to anybody that I was portly or wrinkled. The best thing about our old apartment was that my grandparents had an apartment in the same building. I used to spend a lot of time at their place.

My grandmother likes everyone to call her "Old One," and she's always saying things like, "Listen well, young one!" and "Mark well, my child!" She believes that everyone ought to eat only raw food, except meat, which she believes nobody should eat at all. She spends all her time grinding up nuts and wheat berries and soybeans, and mashing them together with honey and raisins and stuff. It tastes better than it sounds. My grandfather likes to be called "Grandfather." He has this parrot named Lucky, and he's always fooling with him—spraying him for mites, or bathing his feet, or just walking around with Lucky on his shoulder. Both my grandparents eat basically what Lucky eats.

There are some other people living in my grandparents' apartment. Madame Zelatnowa is a friend of my grandmother's. She is an anthropologist and she comes from Europe. She is studying the people of the Himalayas, especially their cooking. When my grandmother isn't dishing out her ground-up stuff, Madame Zelatnowa is making things like roasted barley floating in strong tea with melted butter and scallions. This stuff tastes worse than it sounds.

Some people come and go. Great-uncle Boris lives there in the wintertime. Uncle Boris is a movie nut. He takes 8-millimeter movies of clouds and squirrels in the park. Once he took a bus all over the country and took pictures of the sky in every state in the Union except Alaska and Hawaii.

I used to hang out in my grandparents' apartment as often as I could. The thing I liked about it was that everyone there didn't treat me in any special way. They were all sort of interested in various things, and they would talk to me about them in just the same way they would talk to anybody. Not being able to drop in at my grandparents' apartment was probably the worst thing about moving to the new house.

I was thinking about all this when I heard the electric radio-controlled garage door open. This was a special gadget of my father's. He had it installed the first week we had the new house. There was a button on the dash-board of his car. When he got within two blocks of the house, he'd push the button, and a little radio transmitter under the hood would start an electric motor in the garage that would open the door. When he got inside, he'd push the button again, and the door would close. Sometimes the door would open and close by itself, as trucks with two-way radios went by.

Melvin struggled to his feet and stumbled off to say hello to my father, yawning. My father always got a bigger welcome than I did. I heard the back door slam twice, and Melvin dragged himself back into my room, still yawning, and settled down to sleep again. I knew what had happened—my father had come out of the garage, stepped through the back door, kissed my mother, pat-ted Melvin on the head, taken off his coat, and hung it on a hook, first taking his apron off the hook. The apron had WHAT'S COOKING? printed on the front, and a pic-

ture of a guy in a chef's hat standing in front of a barbecue with a big cloud of smoke coming up from it. Next,
my father had gone outside (that was the second slam)
and started building a fire in the portable barbecue. This
had been going on all summer.

He would pour some charcoal out of a bag, spray about
a gallon of starter fluid over it, and throw in a match.
Then he would stand around for maybe an hour, watching
to see that the fire didn't go out, and blowing on it once
in a while to keep it hot.

Meanwhile, my mother would be in the kitchen, getting the meat ready—steaks or hamburgers or chicken.
At the same time, Melvin's liver would be cooling on the
counter. When the fire was ready, my father would holler to my mother, and my mother would holler to Melvin
and me. While we were making our way to the table, she
would run outside and give my father the hamburgers or
whatever, and then she would run inside and put Melvin's
dish of cool cooked liver down. Then she would run
outside again and get the first of the hamburgers off the
fire from my father. Then she would run in and give one
to me. Then my father would come in, wearing his apron,
with a big long fork in one hand and holding a platter
with the rest of the hamburgers in the other, and we
would all eat supper.

Besides the hamburgers or steak, we would have salad. My parents had been to a restaurant where they
served this special salad with chopped hard-boiled egg
on it, and anchovies, and all sorts of stuff. The waiter
makes the salad at the table, and he has these oversized
pepper mills and salt shakers made of wood, and he does
a whole routine with the salad. Anyway, my father had
gotten the same kind of wooden salt and pepper shakers
and the same kind of big stainless steel salad bowl, and
he would go through the whole routine every night.
Before we moved to the new house I had always liked
hamburgers and things like that. Now I was getting
bored—my parents weren't, though.

"How do you like your new school, son?" my father asked.

"It's OK," I said.

"Have you made any new friends?"

"None of the kids will talk to me."

"Well, it's always hard the first day in a new school," my father said. "You'll make friends."

"I don't think so," I said.

"You say that none of the children will talk to you," my mother said. "Have you tried to talk to any of them?" I didn't say anything. I didn't know how to tell my mother the snotty kids at Bat Masterson Junior High School were sure to think I was a creep.

"To have a friend, be a friend," my mother said. "You just walk up to the other children and say, 'Hi! My name is Leonard Neeble,' and you'll see how quickly you'll get to know some very nice people." I could just imagine how that would go over. "Now, promise me you'll do that, Leonard," my mother said "I don't want you to develop any complexes. You had lots of friends in the old neighborhood."

3

Walking to school the next day, I thought over my mother's suggestion. After all, the kids at Bat Masterson couldn't be all that bad. Maybe I just needed to give them a chance. Maybe I was being too sensitive. After all, only a few kids had giggled at me, not all of them. I decided I would try to be friendly.

I had been assigned to a homeroom, Room 107. Every day at the beginning and end of school I had to go to Room 107. There was a teacher there, Miss Steele. She would be my homeroom teacher all through junior high school. In our homeroom period, which was about fifteen minutes, Miss Steele would read us announcements and help us with our problems—that's what they told me in the office when I was filling out cards. I went to Room 107 and found a seat.

"That's my desk, little boy," someone said. It was a girl about six feet tall. "Now get out of here so I can sit with my friends."

Most of the girls were taller than me, but this one was really a giant. I thought I'd try out my friendly stuff. "Hi! My name is Leonard Neeble," I said. "I didn't know that seats had been assigned."

"Just get out of here, you little pimple," she said.

I took another seat in the back of the room. The giant girl sat down at the desk and leaned forward, talking to a bunch of other girls, all of whom were taller than me.

I watched kids drift into Room 107. They all seemed to know each other. They waved and smiled and changed seats so they could be near their friends. Obviously, seats had not been assigned. That big dopey girl could have just asked me to change seats. I was sitting in the last seat in the last row, so I could see everything that happened in the room.

A teacher came in. She was tall and sort of old. She smiled at the class with her lips pressed together. The bell rang.

"Class, come to order!" Miss Steele said. Everybody sort of shuffled around in their seats. "Now get ready for the P.A. announcements," Miss Steele said.

The door opened, and a little kid came in. He was a lot shorter than me, and was wearing brand-new blue jeans with the cuffs turned up about halfway to his knees. He had these real thick glasses that made his eyes look like fish in a bowl. He looked like he was about six years old.

Then I heard chimes—*bong, boing, boinng*—it was the P.A., the public-address system. There was a big loudspeaker on the wall of the classroom, up near the clock. "WELCOME TO YOUR SECOND DAY OF THE FALL TERM AT BAT MASTERSON JUNIOR HIGH SCHOOL," a voice said. "THIS IS MR. WINTER, YOUR PRINCIPAL. I TRUST YOU ARE ALL SETTLING DOWN TO WORK IN YOUR CLASSES, AND I HOPE WE CAN ALL ENJOY THIS TERM TOGETHER. HOWEVER, NOBODY IS GOING TO ENJOY THIS TERM IF WE HAVE THE SAME PROBLEM IN THE SCHOOL YARD WITH WASTEPAPER AND CANDY WRAPPERS THAT WE HAD LAST TERM. YOU CHILDREN ARE PRIVILEGED TO LIVE IN THE GREATEST COUNTRY IN THE WORLD, AND TO GO TO A SCHOOL WHICH HAS A BEAUTIFUL CAMPUS WHICH HAS JUST BEEN RESURFACED WITH BLACKTOP. THERE ARE WASTEBASKETS EXACTLY EVERY TWENTY FEET IN OUR LOVELY LUNCH COURT, AND THERE ARE BENCHES, ALL FRESHLY PAINTED, FOR YOU TO SIT ON IN THE FINE WEATHER AND ENJOY YOUR LUNCH. THE

BENCHES ARE FOR SITTING—NOT FOR STAND-
ING ON, AND CERTAINLY NOT FOR CARVING AND
DEFACING. AND THE WASTEBASKETS ARE FOR
YOUR WASTEPAPER AND REFUSE. YOU WILL SEE
SOME OF YOUR FELLOW STUDENTS WEARING
ARMBANDS IN ORANGE AND GREEN, OUR
SCHOOL COLORS.—THESE ARE LUNCH COURT
MONITORS, AND I EXPECT YOU TO LISTEN TO
THEM. IF A LUNCH COURT MONITOR TELLS YOU
TO PICK UP A CANDY WRAPPER, YOU WILL PICK
THAT CANDY WRAPPER UP! THE LUNCH COURT
MONITOR HAS THE AUTHORITY TO REPORT YOU
TO THE LUNCH COURT TEACHER, AND THE
LUNCH COURT TEACHER HAS THE AUTHORITY
TO SEND YOU TO MY OFFICE. NOW, MY OFFICE
IS OPEN TO ALL STUDENTS ALL THE TIME TO
DEAL WITH LEGITIMATE PROBLEMS, BUT I
DON'T WANT TO SEE ANY STUDENT IN MY OF-
FICE BECAUSE OF A VIOLATION OF THE LUNCH
COURT CODE. . . ."

He went on like that. It was impossible to listen. Kids
were talking to each other, and Miss Steele was writing
in her attendance book. I decided to try out my friendliness
on the little kid next to me. "Hi!" I said. "My name is
Leonard Neeble."

"Yeah, I know," said the kid. "You're the weirdo. I
saw you in gym class yesterday."

"You there! In the last seat! No talking! Stand up!
What's your name?" Miss Steele was shouting at me.

My name got the usual laughs. Miss Steele went on
about how we are all supposed to listen to the P.A. and
did I think I was a special character. In the background,
Mr. Winter was still booming away on the loudspeaker.
" . . . WE ALWAYS SHOW CONSIDERATION FOR
OTHERS BY KEEPING TO THE RIGHT WHEN PASS-
ING THROUGH THE HALLS, AND WE DO NOT
WEAR SHOES WITH METAL TAPS. ANY BOY
WEARING SHOES WITH METAL TAPS MAY BE RE-

PORTED BY THE HALL MONITOR, WHO WILL
HAVE THE RIGHT TO SEND HIM TO MY OFFICE,
WHICH IS ALWAYS OPEN TO ANY STUDENT WITH
A LEGITIMATE PROBLEM, BUT I DON'T WANT TO
SEE . . ." It went on until the bell rang.

I went to my first class, which was English. Apparently,
the day before, when I hadn't been there, the teacher
had the class write a composition on what they did on
their summer vacation. Today she was going to have the
kids read their papers. Since I didn't write one, I felt safe
in my seat at the back of the room. Several kids were
chosen to get up and read their papers. All of them had
been somewhere. Some of them had been to summer
camps, fancy ones that specialize in dance or tennis or
horseback riding. One kid had gone to Europe on a tour
for kids, and another one had gone with his folks.

The teacher's name was Miss Trumbull, and she seemed
fairly nice. "We have one new boy in class," she said,
"who hasn't written a paper, but maybe he'll tell us about
his summer anyway. Leonard Neeble?"

There was the giggling. Kids swiveled around to see
who Leonard Neeble was.

"Leonard, wouldn't you like to come to the front of the
room and tell us about your summer vacation?" Miss
Trumbull asked.

My face felt hot. I went to the front of the room.
"Well, my parents and I moved to a new house," I said.

"That's very nice," Miss Trumbull said. "And what
else happened to you over the summer?"

"I got a dog," I said.

"Oh, how lucky for you," Miss Trumbull said. "What
kind of a dog is it, Leonard?"

"What kind?"

There was something creeping into Miss Trumbull's
voice that told me she was getting the idea I was feebleminded and needed to be helped along. "Is it a poodle or
a dalmation or a scottie, Leonard?" she said.

"No, it's, he's just a big brown dog—we got him at the

pound." There was silence. I couldn't see the kids in the class—I was looking at the floor.

"Don't mumble, Leonard," Miss Trumbull said. "Did anything else happen during the summer that you'd like to tell us?"

"Well, I worked," I said.

"Oh, you had a job. That's wonderful," Miss Trumbull said. "Would you like to tell us what sort of job it was?"

"Just helping my father in his business."

"And what sort of business is it, Leonard?" I had the feeling Miss Trumbull thought I didn't know how to talk, and she was going to teach me right then and there. Her voice was sort of extra sweet, and she was sort of leaning forward and bending around so she could stand behind me and look at my face at the same time.

"It's a rag business," I said. "Different peddlers bring rags, and my father buys them, and we weigh them and sort them, and pack them in bales, and sell them to factories and places." I was picking up speed. "I sort of liked working there, except a couple of times I got fleas."

"Thank you very much, Leonard, for telling us about your interesting summer. You may return to your seat." Miss Trumbull was standing a good way behind me. All the kids were scratching themselves, like they had fleas, and making chimpanzee faces as I walked to the back of the room.

I don't remember too much about the rest of the day. I gave up on trying to be a friend to have a friend, and spent the lunch period by myself. One kid did talk to me—a lunch court monitor made me pick up a Three Musketeers wrapper that wasn't mine. I didn't say anything to him. I just picked it up and carried it to one of the wire wastebaskets placed every twenty feet, and dropped it in.

After lunch I went to my gym class. As I walked through the door of the gym, I heard this terrifically loud voice shout, "FATSO, WHERE ARE YOUR GYM SHOES?"

4

Because I didn't have any gym shoes, I wasn't allowed to take part in the class. I had to sit on the bleachers at the end of the gym. Mr. Jerris ignored me, which was nice. The other kids all had to climb ropes. They had to shinny up these big fat ropes that hung down from the ceiling. They had to climb up about twenty feet, and then come down without sliding and getting rope burns on their legs. Some of them slid down too fast and got big red marks on the insides of their thighs. I decided to leave my brand-new gym shoes at home in my closet for as long as possible.

For a few days, Mr. Jerris would ask me where my gym shoes were. I would look at the floor and sort of shake my head, and look like I was really sad that I had forgotten my gym shoes. After a while, Mr. Jerris decided that I was stupid or feebleminded or something, and he quit asking me. When I came into the gym class, he would just nod in the direction of the bleachers, and I would climb up and sit down for the rest of the class. It was that way in all my classes. I found out if I acted dumb, pretty soon the teachers would leave me alone. I left all my books and stuff in my locker. When a teacher would ask me where my books were, I'd say I didn't know. Then they'd get me a new book, and I'd leave that in my locker too, and after a while, they just left me alone. After a couple of weeks of school, all I had to do was walk from class to class with nothing in my hands.

The only trouble was, it was boring. If I brought something to read, the teachers might have caught on that I wasn't really stupid. All I had to do was sit and think, and watch the other kids. I got to know a lot about them. I used to wonder what would happen to a kid who really was as dumb as I was pretending to be. Nobody would help him, and he would just sit there like I was doing.

The kids ignored me or maybe giggled at me. The teachers ignored me or just sort of smiled sweetly as if to say, "Leonard, if you will just sit still, and not make any noise, and not take up any of my valuable time, everything will be just fine." Bat Masterson was really a lousy school, even if most of the kids were rich and neat and unwrinkled and tall and didn't wear glasses.

There were a few kids who weren't really in much better shape than I was, like the small one whose name was Henry Bagel. Those kids got ignored and giggled at, and the teachers sort of overlooked them because they didn't look like Bat Masterson students—I mean, they were messy or freakish or smelly or twitchy. I thought at first that they would be willing to be friends with me—if nobody else was looking—but they all wanted to be regular Bat Masterson kids. They didn't want to be seen with me or any of the other weirdos, and they kept trying to be accepted by the real kids. I used to watch them in the lunch court. Each freak had picked out a little group to hang out with, and he would keep trailing after them and laughing at their jokes, and every once in a while he'd shout out something funny he'd been planning to say all week. Sometimes the older kids would stop ignoring Henry Bagel long enough to insult him or make fun of him—and I swear, Henry Bagel looked as though he liked it!

The strange thing was that Henry Bagel and the other weird kids all hated me. The real kids just didn't pay any attention to me, but the freaky kids that everybody played jokes on and punched around really hated me. I think it was because I was the only thing lower than they were. I used to spend time trying to pick the one who would be the lowest person in the school if I dropped dead.

After my boring day in school, I would take all my books home and read them. I am a good reader—since the first grade, when I bought a *Batman* comic and managed to read the whole thing, every word. I wanted to read it all because it was *my* book—I had paid for it. Also it was a lot more interesting than those dumb readers they gave us. Once I smashed my way through that *Batman*, I wasn't afraid to read anything. So I read whatever I wanted.

It only took me a couple of weeks to read all my textbooks. My social studies book I read in one night. In school, the kids had to read a chapter a week—or the teacher would say, "Tonight read pages 93 through 97 inclusive," and the kids would all go "Awwwwww," as though they had just been asked to crawl ten miles on their hands and knees. Then, the next day, the teacher would spend forty-five minutes trying to get the kids to explain what they had read. They could hardly do it. Almost all of them had a reading problem, and those that didn't hated reading because the other kids did.

Mostly what the teacher did was try to get some clue that the kids had read what they were supposed to, and that they understood it. "Who can tell me the name for the holy wars that the knights in the Middle Ages went to fight?" the teacher would ask. No hands. "Anybody?" Finally, a hand. Then the teacher would sort of move her lips silently, saying along with the kid, "Crusades?" Actually, I found that medieval stuff really interesting, and took a lot of books about it out of the public library. There was this good movie with Tony Curtis on TV, and then it turned out that it had been taken from a book, *Men of Iron*, which was even better. I found a lot of good stuff about knights and jousting and Crusades and all that. It was pretty exciting—but not to the kids at Bat Masterson.

To them it was having to pick their way through pages 93
to 97, inclusive—Awwwwww.

The only class I went to where the kids enjoyed
themselves—or admitted they were enjoying themselves—was Mr. Jerris's gym class. They sure loved to
climb those ropes. Mr. Jerris told them one time that
anybody who got an A in gym would be able to pass basic
training in the Marine Corps. After that they went at
those ropes like madmen. I guess they all wanted to be
marines.

My parents are sort of dumb—I mean, I love them
and all that, but they aren't very interesting. They are
only interested in getting things for the house, and barbecuing, and that sort of thing. You can't talk to them the
way you can talk to my grandparents. We'd go over there
every week or so, and it was my only chance to enjoy
some conversation.

Also, I could go outside and meet up with the kids in
the old neighborhood. It wasn't the same as if I'd been
going to school with them every day, but we could still
hack around and tell jokes and throw a ball around. My
former best friend, Charley Nastrovsky, had a new best
friend, Billy O'Brian, who had been my second-best friend,
which was only reasonable, because I wasn't there every
day anymore—but it wasn't quite the same as it had
been before we moved. I mean, they had special jokes
about teachers I had never seen, and that sort of thing.
Still, it was nice to be with people who liked me.

5

"Some school. You could cast a horror movie with some of the kids around here." Somebody was talking to me. I was sitting on my favorite bench at the far end of the lunch court. There wasn't anybody near me except this kid I'd never seen before. He had a beard! I don't mean he had a real beard like a hippie—but he had a heavy stubble like a grown man. He was wearing a green sweater with three yellow stripes around one arm and a big yellow letter *K* on the pocket. It was one of these sweaters that buttons down the front.

"Are you talking to me?" I asked. Nobody had talked to me for weeks.

"Yeah, how can you stand this place? Everybody is so snotty and stupid.—By the way, my name is Alan Mendelsohn."

"Leonard Neeble," I said.

"Glad to meet you, Leonard," Alan Mendelsohn said. I noticed he was wearing black-and-white saddle shoes. I had never seen a real kid wearing those.—I only knew about them from old movies. He also had these weird plaid socks. I could see that Alan Mendelsohn wasn't going to fit in at Bat Masterson Junior High School. In his way he was as outlandish-looking as I was.

"I ought to tell you, I'm sort of a leper," I said. "If anybody sees you talking to me, people are going to treat you as if you had the plague."

That came from the stuff I had been reading about the Middle Ages. There were these lepers—they wore cloaks with hoods, and they had to ring a bell all the time. When anybody heard them coming, they'd get out of the way. I used to pretend that I was one of those lepers, that I had a bell, and that everybody stayed away from me because they were scared of catching leprosy. It was easy to pretend.—Except for the bell, things were just about like that.

"You mean these other slobs don't like you?" Alan Mendelsohn said. "Tell me what you did to get them that way, and I'll do it too."

"You have nothing to worry about," I said. "All you have to do is not look just like everybody else, and you're instant garbage."

"I figured something like that," Alan Mendelsohn said. "These kids have the mental power of a bunch of dandelions. We ought to be able to have some fun with them. Watch that guy walking across the yard."

Alan Mendelsohn pointed to a kid walking across the lunch court eating a sandwich. The waxed paper was sort of waving in his face. He was eating and walking fairly fast toward one of the garbage cans placed every twenty feet. Alan Mendelsohn put two fingers in his mouth, and just as the kid was about two paces away from the garbage can, Mendelsohn whistled. It was the loudest whistle I had ever heard. It traveled in the direction of the kid's head, as though Mendelsohn had thrown a hardball at him. I could almost see the whistle whiz across the lunch court at the kid. The kid looked around with his mouth full of peanut butter and jelly sandwich. He was still walking at the same rate. Turning in the direction of the whistle altered his course just enough to send him smack into the garbage can, which went over. The kid went with it, his legs tangling with the rolling can. He wound up sprawling in a heap of half-eaten sandwiches, wrappers, and banana peels.

"How did you do that?" I asked. The bell rang, ending lunch period.

"I'll show you tomorrow," Alan Mendelsohn said. "Meet

you here." And he raced off, doing a neat hurdle over the kid who was still on his hands and knees amid the garbage.

It turned out that Alan Mendelsohn came from The Bronx, which is part of New York City. His father had been transferred to a new job in Hogboro, and Alan's family had moved into a house in the suburb of West Kangaroo Park, which is where Bat Masterson Junior High School is located. Alan Mendelsohn missed The Bronx in pretty much the same way that I missed the old neighborhood in Hogboro. We started meeting at lunchtime. Alan tried to teach me his special "missile whistle" but I wasn't too good at it. We started to hang out after school. We became friends.

Alan Mendelsohn was a lot less shy than me. Although, as I had predicted, all the Bat Masterson kids shunned him, Alan talked to them anyway. He got into a lot of fights. If someone said something that he thought was insulting, Alan might just top them with another insult—or he might haul off and hit them in the mouth. He knew about a hundred ways to trip people, or to distract them and make them trip themselves—on a bench, a garbage can, or another person. Certain kids who were easy to distract were Alan's special victims. Every time he saw them, he would trip them in a different way. One day he would use the "missile whistle," another day he'd call the kid's name, another day he'd just stick his foot out and trip the kid. He had a couple of trips that I wasn't able to figure out—he'd just walk alongside of a kid and then turn sharply away, and the kid would go over. A couple of kids got to be so scared of Alan Mendelsohn that they'd just trip all by themselves when they saw him coming.

People had looked down on me and ignored me. They started that way with Alan Mendelsohn, but it wasn't long before they hated and feared him. Also he was a good student. He refused to let the teachers ignore him. He talked a lot in class, and always got out of his seat and stood while answering a question or talking. The Bat Masterson kids didn't do that. If they were forced to talk in class, they did it sitting down. Sometimes Alan would pace up and down in the aisle when he was speaking, and once in a while he would even work his way to the front of the room, and pace up and down in between the teacher and the front row of seats. The teachers had to call on him all the time, because the other kids almost never put their hands up. In any class where Alan Mendelsohn was enrolled, you were sure to hear from him about as much as you heard from the teacher.

Another thing Alan did in classes was to find out weird things about the subject that the teacher never knew. Once he started talking about Benjamin Franklin's sex life, and when the teacher shut him up he brought in all these books the next day to prove that everything he had to say was true. There was a big shouting match between Alan and the teacher, and it ended with Alan being sent to the principal's office. He got sent there a lot.

I don't want to give the impression that Alan was mean or a bully. He was always friendly, even after he had beaten someone up. He thought most of the kids at Bat Masterson were stupid, and he liked to trip them and play tricks on them, but he never hated them the way they hated him.

Alan had a judo book, and most days after school we'd go to my house or his house, which was just like mine, and practice flipping each other. We also tried to teach Melvin to trip people, but it was no use.

Alan had over two thousand comic books. He kept them in a bunch of old wire milk-bottle cartons. He had a big notebook in which he wrote down all the numbers and titles of the comics he owned. Alan used to go to all sorts of secondhand bookstores when he lived in The Bronx. He'd pick up old comics and other books he liked.

There weren't any secondhand bookstores in West Kangaroo Park, and Alan said he missed them. We planned a trip to Hogboro to look for bookstores.

I felt a lot better about things in the new school, now that I had a friend. Alan and I had saved up a few weeks' allowance and leftover lunch money for our book-buying trip. Then report cards came out. Mine came with a letter from Miss Steele, my homeroom teacher—it was to my parents. It seemed I was failing everything.

6

The next few days were full of trouble. My parents had to go to school and talk with Miss Steele and the school guidance counselor, a person I had never met. They decided to give me some tests to find out what variety of feeblemindedness I had. The guidance counselor was named Mr. Heinz. He was a nice guy. He told me his whole story the first time I went to see him. It seems he had started out as the wood-shop teacher, but when Bat Masterson needed a guidance counselor, they picked him. So Mr. Heinz took all these courses in psychology and counseling. He took them by mail, from a correspondence school in Ohio.

Mr. Heinz had a lot of tests in his office. They were more like games than tests. He had blocks you put together while he timed you, and pictures of scenes that he would show you—and you had to make up a story about what's going on. He also gave me the inkblot test, which I had heard about, and a lot of other tests—me drawing pictures, and writing things, and filling in blanks. I was excused from classes four afternoons in a row, and every day I went down to Mr. Heinz's office to take tests. Mr. Heinz also gave me gum and candy when I was in his office.

After we had finished all the tests, Mr. Heinz said, "Well, I'm not supposed to tell you the results of the tests, but I will tell you that you are one hundred percent normal and average in every respect. Maybe you're a little bit brighter than average. I'll have a talk with your parents."

I was sorry the tests were over. It was the first time I hadn't been bored since I came to that school.

This is what my parents and Mr. Heinz decided: Since I wasn't feebleminded, and the psychological tests hadn't shown any signs that I was crazy, there was no reason that I should be failing all my subjects. Mr. Heinz said that there had to be something wrong with me, and since he couldn't find out what it was, my parents ought to send me to a child psychologist. Mr. Heinz said we were very lucky, because he could recommend someone really good. It seems the guy who had been his professor-by-mail when he was studying to be a guidance counselor had come to Hogboro and set up an office. He gave my parents the name and telephone number of the professor-by-mail, and they made an appointment for me.

The next Monday, I went to the office of Dr. Prince. It was in a big office building in Hogboro. I had to leave school early to catch the bus—Mr. Heinz had arranged it.

There was a newsstand in the lobby of the office building. I don't know why I did it, but before going up to Dr. Prince's office I bought a piece of bubble gum and a nickel cigar. Alan Mendelsohn had told me that if you chew bubble gum at the same time as smoking a cigar, it won't make you sick. I planned to go somewhere after my appointment with Dr. Prince and have a smoke.

Dr. Prince had his tweed suit that looked too big for him. He wore glasses. There were two big upholstered chairs in his office, the kind you sink into. He told me to sit in one. "You smoke, I suppose," he said. I said sure. "Well, you can smoke here. You can also say dirty words. Anything you say to me, I will never tell anyone. That's called confidentiality."

Actually, I had never smoked so far—the cigar was going to be my first attempt—but I wanted to get off on the right foot with Dr. Prince, so I popped the bubble gum in my mouth, and chewed it up for a while, and then got the cigar started. Mendelsohn was right as usual. I didn't get sick.

"Now suppose you tell me why you hate your parents," Dr. Prince said. As I mentioned before, my parents are sort of dumb, but totally loveable. I didn't hate them, and I told Dr. Prince so.

"Of course, I expected you to say that," Dr. Prince said. "You aren't willing to admit it now, but when you feel more comfortable with me, you will be able to say that you hate your parents." Dr. Prince seemed sort of disappointed. I didn't want to hurt his feelings—after all, he was letting me smoke my cigar, and he had told me that I could say dirty words. He was obviously trying very hard to get me to like him. I wanted to help him out.

"Well, I do feel sort of angry at my parents sometimes," I said.

"Aha! Now we're getting somewhere!" Dr. Prince said. "You're angry at them because they pay more attention to your little sister, right?"

"I don't have a little sister," I said.

"Little brother, then?"

"No. No little brother."

"Older brother? Older sister?"

"No."

"Twin?"

"No."

Dr. Prince looked puzzled. He had a big folder in his lap. I recognized some of the tests Mr. Heinz had given me. Dr. Prince thumbed through the papers in the folder. "I suppose you're upset because your parents drink so much," he said.

I told him that my parents hardly ever drink at all. Dr. Prince was silent for a long time. He stared at the pile of papers in his lap. Finally he said, "We won't get anywhere until you decide to cooperate. You can sit there smoking that cheap cigar and chewing bubble gum and resisting the therapy as long as you like—I don't care—I get paid just the same. But you are not going to be able to solve any of your problems unless you are willing to talk about them."

I started to tell Dr. Prince about how I was mad at my parents sometimes because I didn't like the new house or the new neighborhood or the new school, but he interrupted me.

"Don't rationalize. Right now you are feeling anger at me. It's perfectly normal. I have guessed your secrets, and naturally you want to cover up. You'll understand all this better later on. Now let's talk about something else. How did you feel about things in general when you were six months old?"

I told Dr. Prince that I couldn't remember anything about being six months old. He brightened up a bit when I said that, and he made some notes on a pad.

"Oh? Can't remember? Is that so? Well, don't worry, Leonard. You won't be having any more nightmares before very long. You're pretty confused, but it isn't too late to help you. Come again next Monday at the same time."

I don't think I've ever had a bad dream. When I dream about science-fiction monsters and things like that, I usually enjoy it. I had already caught on that it wouldn't do any good to tell that to Dr. Prince. He shook hands with me, and I went down in the elevator.

I bought another cigar and another piece of bubble gum at the newsstand in the lobby. When I got home, the charcoal in the barbecue was already red-hot. My mother wanted to know how my appointment with the doctor had gone.

"Dr. Prince says it's all right for me to smoke cigars," I said.

7

I listened in on the extension when my parents called Dr. Prince. "Your boy is flunking everything in school, and you're worried if he smokes a cigar?" Dr. Prince shouted. "Let him do what he wants—he's a seriously disturbed child. Just pray that I'm able to save him."

"But won't smoking stunt his growth?" my mother asked.

"Who knows?" Dr. Prince said. "But think about this—would you rather have him short or crazy? By the way, don't call me anymore—it undermines the boy's confidence in me. Get your own psychologist."

That settled the matter of smoking. The conditions were that I was allowed to smoke only in the house, and not in front of company. The next day after school, I invited Alan Mendelsohn over for milk and cookies and cigars. Alan was very impressed that I was seeing a shrink. He said he'd always wanted to go. There was a kid in his old school who went to a shrink. He could come in late, and leave early, and go to the nurse's office and take a nap, and skip gym, and nobody said a word. Alan's parents didn't believe in psychology. I told him that was too bad.

I thought about what Alan said about the kid in his old school. Mr. Heinz knew I was seeing Dr. Prince, and he would be sure to notify my teachers. I could see possibilities arising from seeing Dr. Prince.

My mother had been worried that the other kids would

find out I was seeing a shrink and ostracize me. She still didn't understand that they couldn't ostracize me any more than they did already. *Ostracize* is a word I picked up from my social studies book. It seems that in ancient Greece, once a year, they would all drop pieces of broken pottery into a jar. The pieces of pottery were called *ostrakons*. If you didn't like somebody, you just wrote his name on your *ostrakon*. If he got enough votes, he'd be kicked out of town. The kids at Bat Masterson couldn't kick me out of town, but they could refuse to have anything to do with me—which is what *ostracize* means today. Besides, if they voted on anyone to ostracize it would have been Mendelsohn. He had started something new that seemed to annoy everyone.

It was in the week following my first visit to Dr. Prince that Alan Mendelsohn created his masterpiece. On Thursday he arrived at school very early, before anybody else. As each kid or group of kids arrived, Alan Mendelsohn approached them. "Did you know that I was a Martian?" he asked.

"Huh? What?" the kids would say.

"I'm a Martian—I mean, I'm not exactly a Martian, that is, I was born here on Earth, but my parents were born on Mars, and we go to Mars for our vacations, and someday we're going to move back to Mars to live." Then Alan Mendelsohn would turn and walk away. He kept this up until school started; then he'd catch people in the hall between classes. He'd fall in step with someone, take their arm, and say, "Did you know I was a Martian?"

"Huh? What?"

It went on all day. I hung around after school, waiting for Alan Mendelsohn to walk home with me. He kept starting to leave, but then he'd see another kid he hadn't talked to or didn't remember talking to, and he'd be off. "Say, did I ever tell you that I was a Martian?" I finally got tired of waiting and left. There were very few kids around the school. Alan Mendelsohn was sort of trotting from one kid to another, giving them his message.

That evening the telephone rang. It was Alan, "Say, Leonard, I'm sorry I didn't get a chance to talk to you in school today."

"Yes, well, you seemed pretty busy," I said.

"Indeed I was," Alan said. "I've decided that honesty is the best policy, and I've been letting everyone know who I am; that is, I've been explaining to people that I'm a Martian."

"I heard all about it," I said. "What's the point?"

"Well, Leonard, you see, I actually am a Martian— that is, I myself wasn't born on Mars, but my parents were born on Mars, and we go there all the time, and someday we're going to move back to Mars to live. . . ." Alan had remembered that he hadn't gotten around to me.

I wanted to change the subject. "Are we still going to Hogboro to look for comics and old books on Saturday?" I asked.

"As far as I know, Leonard," Alan Mendelsohn said. "That is to say, if nothing special or catastrophic happens before then."

"I'll see you in school tomorrow," I said.

"Indubitably," Alan said. He had a bunch of books that he had gotten in a secondhand store in The Bronx. They were all about building a mighty vocabulary. Every now and then he would use a word like *indubitably*. We said good-bye and hung up.

I went out into the backyard. My father was hosing down the portable barbecue. "Did you know that Alan Mendelsohn's family are Martians?" I asked. I didn't know why I said that. It was just on my mind.

"I thought his people came from New York," my father said. "It will be too cold to barbecue outside soon, son. Maybe we ought to get one of those electric barbecues and set it up in the kitchen." I went inside the house to get a cigar and read a book on hypnotism that Alan Mendelsohn had loaned me.

The next day, Friday, when I arrived at school, a kid spoke to me, a big kid I had never seen before. "Do you believe?"

"What do you mean?"

"Do you believe he's a Martian?" the big kid asked.

"Sure," I said. The big kid hit me in the stomach and walked away. I felt like I was going to throw up. I sort of staggered over to the building and leaned against the wall, waiting to feel better. Not far away, another kid was approached by a kid carrying one of those green book bags. "Do you believe?" the kid with the book bag asked. "No!" said the other kid, and BANG! the kid swung his book bag and hit the other kid on top of the head.

There were confrontations of this kind going on all over the place. Two kids would meet, exchange a few words, and one kid would bop the other, or they'd shake hands and walk away to find some other kids to question.

The bell rang before things could develop into a full-scale riot, but the kids were in an ugly mood as they crowded into the building, and girls and boys punched, pushed, and shoved one another.

Things were fairly quiet during the morning. There were three of four fistfights in the halls between classes—that was unusual—but nothing big happened. There was a kind of undercurrent of excitement building all morning. Everybody knew that lunchtime was going to be special.

When the bell rang for lunch, there was a loud cheer from all parts of the school. When I got to the lunch court, it was like a battlefield. Trash cans were overturned, benches were lying every which way, garbage was everywhere. Quite a few kids had bloody noses and other minor injuries. Everywhere I heard the question "Do you believe?" "Yes." POW! "Do you believe?" "No!"

POW! Henry Bagel, the smallest kid in our gym class, climbed up the body of Jeb Shore, the biggest kid in our gym class, and knocked him out cold. He had to be carried out on a stretcher by two lunch court monitors.

Girls participated too—in fact it was a girl who blacked my eye when I told her I wasn't sure if I believed or not. Some kids would hit you only if you believed—others hit you if you didn't believe—and some kids would hit you whatever you said.

"Believers over here!" someone shouted, and I was caught in a rushing mob of kids who believed. Someone threw a triple-decker tuna fish sandwich, which hit me in the back of the neck. I looked up and thought I saw Alan Mendelsohn hanging out a second-floor window. He seemed to be enjoying the whole scene.

"Death to the nonbelievers!" someone shouted. Soon a lot of people were shouting it. Across the court were a lot of kids shouting, "Death to the believers!" I was scared. I wanted to get out of there. Some nonbeliever was going to bash my head in a minute.

Then we heard sirens. Three police cars drove right into the lunch court. Other policemen were running from all directions. Mr. Winter, with a policeman on either side of him, was shouting through one of those electric bullhorns, "Go to your homerooms! This is an order! Any student not in his homeroom in five minutes will go to jail!"

School was let out early. Kids had to leave the building a homeroom at a time. There were policemen everywhere. You couldn't hang around the school building —you had to walk out of sight at once. There were squad cars and policemen on foot at every corner for blocks.

8

This is what happened when Alan Mendelsohn was sent to the principal's office after the riot:

"You started a riot!" Mr. Winter said.

"I never did!" Alan Mendelsohn said.

"It was all about you—all about whether you were a Martian or not!" Mr. Winter said.

"Still, I wasn't responsible," Alan Mendelsohn said, "and, the disturbance, or riot, if you want to call it that, was about whether or not people believed I was a Martian."

"Just so," said Mr. Winter. "You convinced some of the students that you were a Martian in order to start a riot."

"I didn't convince them—I simply told them. I told them like this: I am a Martian. My parents were born on Mars. We go to Mars for our vacations, and we will someday go back to Mars to live permanently. What would your reaction be, Mr. Winter, if I had walked up to you and told you that? Would you believe it?"

"Of course I wouldn't believe it," Mr. Winter said.

"Well, neither would I," Alan Mendelsohn said, "so how can you accuse me of planning to start a riot between people who did and did not believe something which I never expected anyone to believe?"

"Why did you tell people you were a Martian in the first place?" Mr. Winter asked.

"Because it's true," Alan Mendelsohn said.

"You are suspended for five days, starting Monday," Mr. Winter said.

"That's fair," Alan Mendelsohn said.

9

Alan Mendelsohn apparently convinced his parents that
the riot wasn't his fault—that is, he had them somewhat
convinced. They still insisted that he stay in the house
for the whole weekend. That put an end to our plans for
a book-buying trip to Hogboro on Saturday. I went over
to Alan's house and hung around for a while on Saturday
morning. He said his parents hadn't put any restriction
on where he went during his week of suspension. They
figured that with me in school he wouldn't have any fun,
since I was the only kid he went around with. He had
mentioned to his mother that he might want to go to the
museum in Hogboro to work on a science project. She
said that would be OK. I said I wished I could be suspended
with him. He said he wished I could too. Alan kept
leafing through comic books, and there wasn't too much
conversation. I told Alan I had to go to the library. He
walked me to the door.

At the door, Alan said, "Leonard, I noticed that you
were with the believers yesterday. Thanks, I appreciate
that."

At the library I found a book in the children's section
called *Psychiatry Made Simple for Younger Readers*. I
checked it out. Also, I took out an adventure book called
Howard Goldberg, Frontiersman. I got home in time for
lunch. Grandfather and the Old One had been invited
over to barbecue in the backyard. When I got there,
they had already arrived. They were sitting in the house
while my father stood over the portable barbecue wear-

33

ing a plaid woolen lumber jacket over his apron. It was really getting kind of cold for cookouts.

"Leonard, are you crazy?" Grandfather asked me when I came through the door.

"No, I'm not crazy," I said.

"See?" the Old One shouted to my mother, who was in the kitchen. She was arranging some alfalfa sprouts the Old One had brought for us to eat. My father was barbecuing chicken for us, and nut cutlets for Grandfather and the Old One. "See, Louise? The boy says he's not crazy. So why are you sending him to a crazy-doctor?"

"He's not a crazy-doctor," my mother shouted back, "he's a child psychologist—and he's helping Leonard adjust so he can do well in school."

Melvin really loved Grandfather. He was sitting in front of him, three-quarters awake, drooling on his knee.

"Phooey!" Grandfather said. "Let the kid join the navy for a couple of years. A few months at sea, and he'll be fine."

"Leonard is only twelve years old," my mother said. "He can't join the navy."

"I was eleven years old when I joined the navy!" Grandfather shouted. "No! Ten years old! I told them I was twenty-three. I had a beard and hair on my chest. I was six feet four inches tall, because I never ate meat, because I never ate chicken, and because I ate almost everything raw. You're cheating your son out of his birthright of good health!"

I wondered how Grandfather could have been six feet four inches tall when he was ten years old. He is about five feet one inch now.

My father came in with the chicken and nut cutlets. My grandparents didn't want to eat the nut cutlets because they were cooked. My father kept insisting. He wanted to show off how good he was at barbecuing.

"Just a few alfalfa sprouts for me," the Old One said, "and some raw potatoes and maybe a little yogurt." All through the meal my father kept trying to get her to taste the nut cutlets.

After lunch we all sat around and Grandfather talked about the Ituri Rain Forest Pygmies. He said they run everyplace, and clap their hands while they're running so they won't surprise a leopard. He also said that if you take Pygmies out of the forest and into the open grassland, they get confused. They aren't used to being able to see more than fifteen or twenty feet away. If they see a bunch of elephants a long way off, they will not think they are elephants that look tiny because they are far away, but little tiny elephants fifteen or twenty feet away. Grandfather said he always wanted to go and visit the pygmies. The Old One said she thought they were so small because of all the meat in their diet. The Old One wasn't much taller than a Pygmy herself—she came up to Grandfather's shoulder.

After a while, my parents took my grandparents home. First, my father showed them how the radio-controlled electric garage-door opener worked. Then they drove off. I had decided not to go along for the ride. I wanted to read my book about psychiatry.

The book was sort of interesting. I read it all evening Saturday, and most of the day Sunday.

School on Monday was more or less back to normal. Mr. Winter made a long speech on the public-address system about how disgraceful everybody's conduct had been. He said the Bat Masterson students had a certain tradition to uphold. He said that for years and years, the Bat Masterson student had been a model to the world of good conduct, courtesy, and correct attire. He was ashamed of us all. And he was especially ashamed that a student who did not have the true Bat Masterson spirit had brought about such shameful behavior on the part of boys and girls who had been brought up to know better. He went on and on as usual. What really got me was that most of the kids acted as if they were really ashamed that they let good old Bat Masterson down.

I was let out early so I could go to my appointment with Dr. Prince. I caught the bus to Hogboro. Once again I bought a cigar at the newsstand in the lobby. This time I bought one called a Fargo Brothers Rum-Soaked Curley-Q. This was a great big cigar that had a wavy shape. It turned out to be a terrific smoke. I didn't even need the bubble gum. It was soaked in some kind of sweet sugary rum, and it made sparks every now and then when you smoked it.

"Well, Leonard, what kind of week have you had?" Dr. Prince asked me, once I was settled into the big chair, my Fargo Brothers Rum-Soaked Curley-Q sparking and burning away.

'I've had a lot of anxiety," I said. I picked this up from the psychiatry book I read over the weekend.

"Anxiety, eh?" Dr. Prince said, leaning forward in his chair. "Tell me more."

"Well, I have these dreams, and I wake up sweating, and sometimes, sometimes I can't tell if it's a dream or not," I said. This was all baloney. I had gotten it from the book too.

"Yes, yes, tell me about these dreams," Dr. Prince said. He was leaning way forward in his chair, he was puffing his pipe very fast, and he had his pen and pad poised, ready to write down whatever I said.

"Well, in these dreams I have missed school, and they come and get me, and it turns out that I wasn't really sick—that is, I didn't have a good excuse—and these people, teachers and principals, all say I have to be punished, and they take me to the electric chair. Then they strap me in, and my parents are there, crying, and the principal gives the order to throw the switch—then I wake up."

Dr. Prince was writing furiously. There were beads of sweat on his forehead. He was puffing his pipe so hard that little showers of sparks and ashes were flying all over the place, and landing in his lap. "So you think you'll be executed if you miss school, do you?" he asked.

"Well, no," I said, sort of hesitating, "I mean, they wouldn't kill me for missing school—would they?"

"Leonard, I want you to take a day off school," Dr. Prince said. "No—take the rest of the week off. Just stay home, or go to the movies, or do whatever you like. I will call Mr. Heinz, the guidance counselor, and explain everything, and he'll call your parents."

"You mean—you mean—not—not go to school?" I tried to sound frightened. "But what will they do to me? I mean, won't my parents, I mean, won't I be punished?"

"Nothing will happen to you, Leonard, my boy," Dr. Prince said. "Obviously, you are so tense about this, it is no wonder you are unable to do well in your classes. You just take the rest of the week off, and don't worry. You may feel a little nervous, but after you return to school and see that nothing happens to you, you will never have to be afraid again—and you won't have those dreams."

"Are you sure?" I said. "I mean, couldn't I just come in late—say five minutes?"

"Trust me, Leonard. Take the week off. It will be easy."

That night I called Alan Mendelsohn and told him I had the rest of the week off. We arranged to meet the next morning on the nine o'clock bus to Hogboro.

10

At eight o'clock the next morning the cow arrived. Actually it was a half-cow. My parents had bought this great big freezer—it had been delivered the week before. With the freezer, at no extra cost, they got a half-cow, butchered and wrapped in white paper packages with what part of the cow it was written on the outside.—For example, *Top round steak* and *Rib roast*. The writing was in black crayon. There were a lot of packages. It took two men a half hour to carry them all inside, and take them down to the basement, and stack them in the freezer.

When my parents told my grandparents about buying the freezer and the half-cow, my grandparents almost went wild. My grandfather wanted to know if my father was going to have the head of the cow stuffed and mounted on a plaque, and hung on the wall.

I wondered if all the meat that made up our half-cow actually came from one animal. If it did, it seemed to me that there might be a certain risk in buying so much meat all at once. I'm not sure if this is so, but it seems to me that all things being equal—such as what the cow was fed, age of cow, breed of cow, and so forth—some cows probably taste better than others. What would happen if you bought a whole half-cow and then found out that it tasted lousy? And what would happen if you went away on vacation, and a fuse blew, and the freezer went dead for two weeks? That actually did happen to us later on, before we were even a quarter of the way through our half-cow. Grandfather thought it was a big joke.

Having a half-cow's worth of beef in the freezer made me think more about the fact that all those white-paper-wrapped packages had been a real live animal, running around and enjoying itself. Before this, I had always thought of meat as something on a plate. I had been on a school trip to a farm once, and I remember that the cows had very nice eyes and tried to lick me with big slurpy tongues. I didn't like being licked, but there was no mistaking their good intentions. I had always thought of cows as nice animals that give milk—and meat as something your mother serves you. There hadn't been any connection before this. Watching the freezer fill up with meat made me realize that my grandparents at least had a point about being vegetarians—although I still couldn't understand why everything had to be raw.

I had a toasted corn muffin and a cup of half milk, half coffee. My mother was watching the men carry the meat to the basement, and checking off the number of parcels of each particular cut of meat on a checklist the freezer company had given her.

I went out to catch the Hogboro bus. Alan Mendelsohn had gotten on a few blocks earlier, near his house. "How come you don't have to go to school?" he asked. I told him that Dr. Prince had given me an excuse for the rest of the week. "God, I wish they'd let me have a psychologist," Alan Mendelsohn said.

It was the same bus I always took to go see Dr. Prince. It went right past Bat Masterson Junior High School. Alan and I punched each other as we rolled past the school. It felt good to be off on an adventure when all the other kids were listening to Mr. Winter on the loudspeaker. Alan was particularly friendly. He didn't say anything about it, but I suspected he'd had a boring time the day before, when he was the only kid out of school and not sick.

The bus ride only took about half an hour. We pulled into the Hogboro bus terminal. The first thing we did was look in the window of the tattoo place near the bus station. There were big sheets of paper with copies of the tattoos you could get. We discussed getting tattooed, but neither of us could find anything we absolutely would like to have on our skin. About the best one was Donald Duck, with the word *Mother* written underneath. We decided to give it more thought.

We walked uptown along Clarkle Street. We had looked in the Hogboro Yellow Pages, and there were a lot of bookstores on Clarkle Street. I had about fifteen dollars, and Alan had about the same. After a few blocks we saw four or five bookstores clustered together in the middle of the block. The biggest one had a vertical sign, as tall as the building. BOOKS, it said, in red block letters.

We went in. The bookstore had a funny smell—not bad, just funny. It was sort of a dry smell, like oatmeal before you cook it. There were bookshelves all the way to the ceiling, which was high, and tables piled with books, and books in stacks tied together with string, and a flight of stairs going up, with a big red arrow pointing straight up. On the arrow was a sign: More Books Upstairs—Comics and Periodicals—Third Floor.

We went up. The third floor was all magazines and comics. There were big tables covered with comics standing upright in long rows. A sign hanging from the ceiling said All Comics 5¢. We began to flip through the comics. Alan had a list with the titles and numbers of the comics he wanted. It was slow work. The only comic he found that was on his list of wants was a copy of *Action Comics* Number 1—but he didn't buy it because there was a corner torn off the cover. He said he only bought comics that were perfect.

I figure that there were about half a million comics in that place, and Alan went through about half of those. I was getting sort of bored. I was happy when Alan said he'd had enough of that place and why didn't we try someplace else. He had gathered together a stack of about fifty comics that he might just possibly consider buying if nothing more interesting turned up. He put them all together under a table, so no one else would be able to buy them until he made up his mind.

We went down the stairs and outside into the street. It seemed very noisy and lively in the street after the quiet of the bookstore.

11

There was a little bookstore next to the one we'd just
come out of. The sign said SAMUEL KLUGARSH—
OCCULT AND ORIENTAL BOOKS. Smaller signs said
Meditation, Hypnosis, Magic, Outer Space, Ghosts, Mind
Control, Healing, and Foot Reflexology. The signs were
yellow with red letters, and they were stuck all over the
front of the store. In the window there were books with
pictures of flying saucers and weird guys with long white
beards and Egyptian stuff on the covers. It was an interesting bookstore.

We started to go in, but the door was locked. There
was a sign taped to the inside of the glass door; it said
Gone to Bermuda Triangle—Leave Messages at Morrie's,
Next Door.

Morrie's was another bookstore on the other side of
Samuel Klugarsh's. It was very small, and the window
was dirty, and there was a lot of dust on everything, and
dead flies. We went inside. Morrie's Bookstore was sort
of crummy. There were crude nailed-together tables along
the walls, with a few beat-up books lying face up on
them, and a metal book rack, with books on both sides of
it, running down the middle of the room. The books had
titles like *Accounting Made Simple* and *The 1952 Nafsu
Oil Company Employees' Yearbook*—stuff nobody could
possibly be interested in. At the back of the store was
one of those redwood picnic tables with redwood benches.
There were three chessboards with games in progress on
the picnic table, but nobody playing—just an old hunch-

backed guy, wearing a cap and steel-rimmed glasses, sleeping stretched over the table.

Near the back of the store, at another table, was a guy with the biggest beard I'd ever seen and one of those handlebar mustaches—the kind they wax—with the ends pointing up. The beard and mustache were all the more impressive because the guy's head was bald. He was wearing a green turtleneck sweater and he had what looked like a brass potato hanging around his neck on a leather thong.

The guy with the beard and bald head was sitting in front of an old typewriter. It was one of those big office machines, all black and shiny, with lots of little knobs and levers sticking out all over it. Next to the typewriter, on one side, was a stack of paper almost as high as the top of the machine. On the other side of the typewriter was another stack of paper about half as high.

The guy with the beard was typing. As we came in, he finished a page, and took it out of the machine, and put it on top of the tall stack. Then he took a sheet of paper from the small stack, and fed it into his machine, and continued typing. He must have had about two thousand pages typed already.

"Gentlemen, welcome to Morrie's Bookstore," the bald beard said. "I am William Lloyd Floyd, resident philosopher. Is there anything I can do for you?"

"Well . . . uh . . . actually . . ." Alan Mendelsohn was a little uneasy for a change. "You see, we . . . we were going to go into Samuel Klugarsh's next door, but the sign on the door said come in here. . . . It said 'Gone to Bermuda Triangle,' so we . . . ah . . . came in here." I don't blame Alan Mendelsohn for being nervous; it was a weird place—not unfriendly or scary, just unlike any place we'd ever been before.

"That's the Bermuda Triangle Chili Parlor, around the corner," William Lloyd Floyd said. "Klugarsh is always eating there. He says their chili beans have sympathetic karma. Actually he's a calorie freak—eats about seven meals per day." William Lloyd Floyd was typing away fast and furious at the same time he was talking to us. "If you've got urgent business, you could go over to the chili parlor and join him. He likes to have company when he eats, although I personally haven't got the stomach to watch him. You aren't Mind Control students of his, are you?"

"No, we just wanted to look around the store," Alan Mendelsohn said.

"Oh, in that case, stick around," William Lloyd Floyd said. "Klugarsh will drop in here on his way back—he shouldn't be gone more than a few minutes." I had gotten close enough to see that William Lloyd Floyd was typing exactly what he had just been saying—also what we had said. The last line he had typed was—*he shouldn't be gone more than a few minutes*.

"Excuse me, Mr. Floyd," I began.

"Call me Bill."

"Excuse me, Bill," I said. "Do you mind if I ask you what you're typing? It looks like a book. Is it?" William Lloyd Floyd typed while I talked—he had been typing the whole time we had been in Morrie's Bookstore.

"Yes, it's a book, all right," he said. I could see what he typed: *Yes, it's a book, all right.* .

"What sort of a book is it?" I asked. "I notice you're typing everything we say."

"Just a second," William Lloyd Floyd said. He had come to the end of a page, whipped it out of the machine, and was putting another one in. "Not only have I typed everything we say," he said, typing it, "but everything anybody has said in here for weeks. Also, I'm typing everything I think, and whenever possible, whatever anybody else thinks when I'm feeling telepathic. In answer to your question about what sort of book this is, it is the ultimate work of fiction and philosophy. It includes everything that has ever happened to me, everything that has ever happened to anybody else that I know of, and everything that is happening right now." *Right now*, the machine clicked.

"How long have you been writing it?" I asked.

"Eight weeks now," William Lloyd Floyd said. "I thought I had it finished five or six times, but someone always comes in and starts saying or thinking something that hasn't been covered yet—and I have to go back to work. These aren't all the pages," he said, pointing at the tall stack next to the typewriter. "I have boxes more at home."

An alarm clock on the table went off. "Whew, I thought lunchtime would never come," William Lloyd Floyd said. "Will you join me for a snack?"

"We wouldn't want to impose," Alan Mendelsohn said.

"Oh, no imposition at all," William Lloyd Floyd said. "I'm just going to send the Mad Guru out for some bread and cheese. Please join me—you're going to wait for Samuel Klugarsh anyway."

"Mad Guru?" Alan Mendelsohn said.

"That's right. My colleague. Oh, Guru! Lunchtime! Wake up!" William Lloyd Floyd shouted, and the old hunchbacked guy woke up.

"What will you be wanting, Chief? The usual?" the old guy asked.

"I think so," William Lloyd Floyd said, "and these two gentlemen will be joining us, so you'd better get the large size Wonder bread. Gentlemen, kindly give the Mad Guru a dollar each—you don't mind contributing toward lunch, do you?"

We each gave the Mad Guru a dollar, and he put on an old greasy raincoat and went out.

"How come you're not typing any of this?" Alan Mendelsohn asked.

"I'm on my lunch break," William Lloyd Floyd said. "Even a great artist has to relax once in a while. I've been working all morning, and I'm bushed."

The Mad Guru was back in just a couple of minutes with a brown paper bag. Out of the bag he took a family-sized loaf of Wonder bread and a chunk of blue cheese. There was a big electric coffeepot, and William Lloyd Floyd poured us cups of black coffee. It was a strange lunch. The coffee was strong, and the blue cheese with it made a funny feeling in the back of my throat. William Lloyd Floyd had turned his chair around and ate sitting near his typewriter. Alan Mendelsohn, the Mad Guru, and I ate at the picnic table with the chessboards.

"You're looking at my potato," William Lloyd Floyd said, fingering the brass lump hanging on the leather thong around his neck. "This is really rare. It's a petrified potato from the moon. I got it from the first man to ever go to the moon—this was years and years before the astronauts. This man was a master of teleportation—he could send himself places by thought, you know. He projected his thoughts to the moon one time and discovered the remains of a lost civilization. He brought back this petrified potato. I traded him a 1961 Volkswagen for it. He wanted to go to San Francisco, and I had this car, and well, there you are. Personally, I think he was a fool to part with this. The astronauts didn't find any potatoes, or if they did, they kept quiet about it. The thing must be worth a couple of million. You don't play chess, do you? It's twenty-five cents a game—seventy-five cents to play against me. The Mad Guru, who is an intergalactic Grand Master, will give you a chess lesson for a dollar and a half."

The skinniest man I ever saw in my life walked into Morrie's Bookstore. He had heavy tortoiseshell glasses and one of those crew cuts that are flat on top. He was wearing a green corduroy jacket and a pink bow tie.

"Ah, Klugarsh!" William Lloyd Floyd said. "These gentlemen have been waiting for you. Allow me to introduce . . . I didn't get your names. . . ."

We introduced ourselves. William Lloyd Floyd made

a note in pencil in the margin of one of his typewritten pages. "You'll be in the index," he said.

"I hope you haven't been waiting long," Samuel Klugarsh said. "Please come with me, and we'll get started at once."

12

We followed Samuel Klugarsh out of Morrie's Bookstore. He unlocked the door to his shop, and we followed him in.

"Klugarsh is sorry you were kept waiting," he said. "You didn't make an appointment, so, of course, I wasn't expecting you."

"Actually, we just wanted to look around," Alan Mendelsohn said.

"That's perfectly all right," Samuel Klugarsh said. "Look at anything you like, while Klugarsh gets the equipment ready."

"Equipment?" I asked.

"The best equipment," Samuel Klugarsh said. "My method of Mind Control is the most scientifically advanced, technologically perfect, and generally successful system of accelerated human growth ever devised by man. . . . Now, where's that extension cord?"

Alan and I looked at each other. Samuel Klugarsh was rummaging around, dragging all sorts of machines, tangles of wire, and rolled-up sheets of paper from under tables. He set up a sort of easel, and dragged a bench into the middle of the room. All over the room there were signs like the ones on the outside of the store, yellow with red lettering. The signs all had slogans like Talk is Cheap—Action is Expensive; and Think Before You Think; and Today is the Yesterday You Won't Be Able To Remember Tomorrow.

Obviously, Samuel Klugarsh was setting up some sort

of lecture or demonstration for us. "Mr. Klugarsh," I said, "we just came in to look at some books—we didn't plan to see your demonstration."

"How do you know that?" Samuel Klugarsh asked. "Do you know what I'm going to demonstrate?"

We admitted that we didn't.

"Well, then, how do you know you don't want to see it? Just look around and entertain yourselves—Klugarsh is almost ready," Samuel Klugarsh said.

There were books about all sorts of weird stuff I had never heard of—bean sprout therapy, messages from flying saucers, ancient health secrets of New Jersey, transcendental yoga, knee manipulation to increase brainpower. There were also a lot of books with pictures of strange-looking guys on the covers—a lot of them had beards—all of them were staring into the camera with this strange expression, eyes open very wide. They had titles like *Harold Platt, New-age Seer of Rochester;* and *Blong! You Are a Pickle! (The Blong-Pickle Master's Guide to Ego Submersion);* and *Fred Watanabe—The Divine Inner Self*.

"Gentlemen, please take your seats. Klugarsh is ready to begin his presentation," Samuel Klugarsh announced.

Alan Mendelsohn and I sat down on the bench, facing Samuel Klugarsh, who was standing in front of the easel. On a table beside him were a bunch of odd-looking machines—square, and made of metal with black crackly paint on it. Some of them had tubes sticking out of the top and black dials with white numerals. On the easel was a great big drawing pad. The cover of the pad was turned back, and the first page showed a picture of what looked like an old-fashioned light bulb. Lettered above the light bulb were the words *Klugarsh Mind Control System*. Under the light bulb it said *Inc*.

"Gentlemen, what you are about to hear and see will be the most astounding and revolutionary set of ideas to which you have ever been exposed. You may not understand everything right away, some of these concepts are very deep. Klugarsh asks you to pay careful attention, and in the interests of time being saved, to please refrain from bursts of applause. Also, kindly try not to faint from astonishment. If you have any questions, Klugarsh will answer them at the end."

Samuel Klugarsh flipped over the page of the big drawing pad. There was a Magic Marker drawing of something that looked sort of like a cauliflower. "Gentlemen, the human brain—the most exquisite mechanism on earth," Samuel Klugarsh said. "This drawing is the result of intensive work by Klugarsh Research Associates, Incorporated. Together with the Klugarsh Foundation, our organization has delved deeper into the secrets of the brain than man has ever done before. It is well known that human beings make use of no more than ten percent of the potential power of the brain. If we were able to use twenty percent or even fifteen percent of our brainpower, we would all be geniuses and go down in history. There is no way to imagine what a human being would be able to do if he could utilize one hundred percent of his brainpower. Please keep this in mind during the rest of our little talk."

I couldn't understand why it took Klugarsh Research Associates and the Klugarsh Foundation such intensive work to make the Magic Marker cauliflower/brain drawing. It looked like an ordinary cartoon to me.

Samuel Klugarsh flipped the page. There was a complicated drawing with all sorts of funny symbols connected by lines. It looked sort of like a schematic diagram of a radio or stereo set. I had seen one of those—it came with the stereo that was also a bar that my parents had bought for the living room in the new house. It was like one of those old-fashioned globes of the world, a big one, that stands on the floor. You lifted the top half back on hinges, and there was your stereo, with AM and FM and a record player and an eight-track tape player; and around the inside edge of the globe were holes to put glasses and bottles into.

"This is a schematic diagram of a simple radio set," Samuel Klugarsh said, "a 1934 RCA Victor radio—this very radio, in fact." He pointed to one of the machines on the table. Old-time radios, that's what they were!

"It doesn't look much like the brain in the first drawing, does it? But in fact, it is very much like that brain—very much indeed. Look at this!" Samuel Klugarsh flipped to the next page, and there was another schematic diagram, only instead of being sort of squared-off, the lines, which were supposed to represent the wires in the radio, were curved. The whole picture had more or less the shape of a cauliflower. "Astounding, isn't it?" Samuel Klugarsh said with a triumphant smile. Samuel Klugarsh had a long wooden pointer, and he pointed to the various symbols in the radio-brain-cauliflower drawing. He didn't say what they were, though.

"Yes gentlemen, astounding . . . but not one-half, not one-tenth as astounding as what I'm going to tell you now. Having discovered the uncanny similarity between the human brain and radio receiving sets, I established the Klugarsh Psychical Phenomena Bureau. I began to collect little bits of information, piece things together, to study, study, study. I found out how to utilize the full one hundred percent of my brainpower. Now, this is the truly amazing part—right now, while we're talking, I'm in direct communication with people on Mars!"

Alan Mendelsohn had been sort of sitting bent over on the bench, with his elbows resting on his knees, during Samuel Klugarsh's lecture. Every now and then, when Samuel Klugarsh wasn't looking, he would poke me in the ribs. However, he was sitting up straight now.

"People on Mars?" he asked.

"Of course," said Samuel Klugarsh. "Long ago, I perfected the art of teleportation, or thought-travel. Then, adding a few little extra details of my own, I developed that art to the point where I am, in effect, in two places at once. In fact, while we are having our very pleasant conversation here on Earth, I am also sitting in the office of the Martian High Commissioner for Extra-Martian Transport, having a friendly chat with my old friend Rolzup, the Deputy High Commissioner. I am aware of my activities on Mars as I talk to you here, and I am aware of my activities on Earth as I sit sipping a cup of fleegix with my friend Rolzup."

"What is Rolzup saying?" Alan Mendelsohn wanted to know.

"I'm afraid I can't tell you that," Samuel Klugarsh said. "Not that it is anything private or secret or confidential—it's only that it just isn't the done thing to carry messages from one world to another. There are certain restrictions of usage that come with extraordinary powers. However, if you decide to learn Klugarsh Mind Control, it won't be very long before you can go to Mars yourself. Rolzup, who is one of my students, and therefore able to monitor our conversation, says it will be his pleasure to receive a visit from you both."

"You have students on Mars?" I asked.

"Oh, yes," Samuel Klugarsh laughed, "many thousands of students. You see, the civilization on Mars is far more advanced than ours. Therefore, they instantly recognized the value of Klugarsh Mind Control. Here on Earth, it's quite another matter. People just aren't ready for the next step forward in evolution. But let me get back to my explanation."

Samuel Klugarsh flipped the page of the big pad again. The next picture looked like a portable transistor radio with some wires coming out of it.

"This is the Klugarsh Mind Control Omega Meter," Samuel Klugarsh said. "Klugarsh has perfected this instrument to help Mind Control students all over this world and others. The principle of the Omega Meter is this: As you know, the brain is constantly putting out electrical impulses. You may have heard of alpha, beta, and theta waves—these are the only ones science has discovered in man, so far. That is, until Klugarsh discovered any number of other brain waves, the most important of all being the omega wave. The omega wave is produced in what I call 'state twenty-six,' which is an incredibly high state of creative consciousness, in which we utilize one hundred percent of our brainpower. The use of the Klugarsh Omega Meter is very simple. It is based on the principle of biofeedback. The meter makes a continuous buzzing noise, except when it receives omega waves. Then a tiny tape recording inside plays a few bars of 'Jingle Bells.' To activate the Omega Meter, we clip one of these wires to each of our earlobes, and meditate fiercely. The buzzing continues until we get to the point where we are producing omega waves. Then we hear the machine play 'Jingle Bells.'

"Once we are able to produce omega waves, we can then do things which we previously thought were impossible—for example, visit Mars. We can also read the thoughts of others, and we can control the actions of others. Of course, all of this takes practice, and you mustn't expect to be able to do it all at once. First you have to learn to make the Omega Meter play 'Jingle Bells.' Then you can learn to control the actions of others—that's the easiest thing. Somewhat later you can learn to read the thoughts of others; and later still, you can learn to do thought-traveling, to cause objects to move, to see into the past and the future, and to accurately predict the weather."

Samuel Klugarsh flipped the page again. The next pictures showed a man with a big smile on his face. "This is a picture of a man who has completed the Klugarsh Mind Control course. As you can see, he is totally happy. This concludes my remarks—now, I will be happy to answer three questions."

13

"Excuse me, Mr. Klugarsh," Alan Mendelsohn said, "but a lot of what you were saying didn't make sense."

"Klugarsh said three questions," Samuel Klugarsh said. "What you said wasn't a question. I'm not interested in your opinions. Try again."

"Excuse me, Mr. Klugarsh," Alan Mendelsohn said, "but a lot of what you said didn't make sense—did it?"

"That's better," Samuel Klugarsh said. "And the answer is no, it didn't make sense to you. That is because you are ignorant. For example, do either of you speak Turkish?"

We both said we didn't.

"*Wake waka. Needle noddle noo. Hoop waka dup dup. Baklava.* That's Turkish," said Samuel Klugarsh. "You didn't understand what I said because you're ignorant of the language. To you it just sounded like gibberish; to a Turk it's the pledge of allegiance—just a matter of point of view."

"I'm sorry," Alan Mendelsohn said, "I didn't mean to put you down."

"There's no need to be embarrassed, my boy," Samuel Klugarsh said. "Ignorance is nothing to be ashamed of—until you find out you've got it. Once you realize you're ignorant, if you don't do something about it, then you have the right to feel ashamed. So you mustn't feel bad that you have just told a great scientist and teacher that he doesn't make sense—twice. You mustn't feel bad because you were speaking out of ignorance. After all, this is America. In some countries, in Iceland for instance, things would be very different—but here we give people a chance!"

Samuel Klugarsh was very red in the face. He was shaking his finger at Alan Mendelsohn, and jumping up and down. We were a little scared of him. Alan kept glancing at me. He wasn't so fresh when he was outside of school. If a teacher had gotten that angry at him, Alan Mendelsohn would have enjoyed it.

"You little snot-noses!" Samuel Klugarsh shouted. "You come in here, and I give you the benefit of my years of study, I show you the exact same lecture that I gave to the president of the United States, and it isn't good enough for you. What kind of parents do you have to let you grow up so impudent? Sit still!"

Alan and I were both thinking about streaking out the door—but how did he know that? Neither of us had moved a muscle.

Samuel Klugarsh seemed to calm down a little. "Sorry I lost my temper, boys," he said, "but when you have devoted as many years as I have to a wonderful idea that is going to save mankind, and so many people don't even give you a chance to explain it to them, well, you get a little sensitive. Look, forget about the other two questions. You look like intelligent kids to me. Since you didn't understand my lecture, what I'll do is give you both the Klugarsh Mind Control course for half the usual price for one student. It usually costs twelve hundred dollars. I'll let you both take it for six hundred. That's three hundred apiece. Guaranteed. If you don't make it to Mars in five years, you get a portion of your money back."

"We don't have six hundred dollars," I said.

"No, I thought you didn't," Samuel Klugarsh said. "What do you say to a hundred and fifty? A hundred? Fifty?" Samuel Klugarsh could see from our faces that he was getting nowhere. "Look, how much can you kids spend?"

Alan and I both still had about fourteen dollars and change, some of which we needed to get back to West Kangaroo Park. "What about twenty-four dollars?" Alan asked.

"Twenty-four dollars? You insult Samuel Klugarsh," Samuel Klugarsh said. "However, I can do something for you for that price—although it isn't as good as taking the whole course. I will give you—*give* you, for twenty-four dollars, a portable Omega Meter and the first volume of the Klugarsh Mind Control course. This takes you through the basic Omega monitoring exercises, into making people do whatever you want. It doesn't deal with reading the thoughts of others or teleportation, and it isn't guaranteed. Still, the regular price is eighty-nine ninety-five—you're saving almost sixty-six dollars. And you can always sell the course to another seeker for forty bucks. What do you say?"

Samuel Klugarsh had dug out and was holding a little green plastic transistor radio with two wires hanging from it. At the end of each wire was a shiny alligator clip. In his other hand was a black plastic three-ring binder. Alan and I looked at each other. I decided I was going to do whatever he did. "We'll take it," Alan said.

Samuel Klugarsh handed us the transistor radio and the binder. The binder had a light bulb stamped in gold, like the one on the first page of the chart he had shown us. You could see where he had painted black over where it had said Hogboro Light and Power Co., and then in white paint had written *Klugarsh Mind Control System, Inc.*

"This Omega meter is disguised as a transistor radio," Samuel Klugarsh said. "See, when you clip it to your ears and turn it on, you will hear a continuous buzzing." He clipped the alligator clips to my ears—it hurt—and turned it on. It buzzed. "When you get so that you can produce omega waves, it will play 'Jingle Bells,' " he said.

"Mr. Klugarsh, clip it on your ears, so we can hear it play 'Jingle Bells' now," said Alan Mendelsohn.

"I'm afraid I can't do that you little . . . fellow," Samuel Klugarsh said. "You see, my omega waves are so strong, they would throw the machine out of adjustment. However, I can show you on my stationary Omega Meter." Samuel Klugarsh pointed to another machine on the table, a big one with tubes and dials all over it. "This one is a little more complicated than yours," Samuel Klugarsh said. He slipped on a leather headband with wires—his machine didn't clip to the lobe of your ear—and pushed a button. The machine played 'Jingle Bells' until he pushed another button to stop it. "You see, I am always in a state of omega wave production," he said.

"Now about the book," Samuel Klugarsh went on, removing his Omega Meter headband. "It will tell you exactly how to use the Omega Meter, so I won't waste time on it now. The book is divided into two sections— Using Your Omega Meter, and the second section, Controlling the Thoughts and Actions of Others. In connection with this, there is a formality of intergalactic law and usage that we must observe. When I point to you, say 'I swear.' Now, I promise never to use my power of mind control to steal money or overthrow the United States government." He pointed. We swore.

Samuel Klugarsh put our Omega Meter and Mind Control course into a brown paper bag, and we handed him our twenty-four dollars. It occurred to me that this was the biggest thing I had ever bought entirely on my own. I mean, my mother has been giving me money to buy my own clothes for a long time—but she tells me how much I can spend on, say a pair of shoes, and tells me what kind to get and where to get them. So things like that don't count. My half of the Omega Meter and Mind Control course, at twelve dollars, was the most expensive thing I had ever purchased by myself. We said good-bye to Mr. Klugarsh and started walking toward the bus terminal.

We were a couple of blocks away from Samuel Klugarsh's bookstore, carrying our package containing the Mind Control course and Omega Meter, when we saw a familiar hunched figure. It was the Mad Guru.

"Mornin' to ye, gentlemen, mornin'," the Mad Guru said, sort of touching his cap and walking sideways. "What bus take ye?"

"Take ye?" I asked—I didn't quite understand.

Alan Mendelsohn did, though. "We're taking the West Kangaroo Park bus," he said, "and where do you get this 'Good morning' stuff? It's two in the afternoon."

"Arrr, the West Kangaroo Park bus is it?" the Mad Guru said. "Waal, some speak of her as an evil bus. Some say that the driver is mad and searches for a white sixty-eight Chrysler. Some say that all who ride in her are doomed—but I say—Mornin' to ye, gentlemen. Mornin', mornin'." The Mad Guru half-backed, half-walked sideways around a corner and out of sight.

"That was spooky," I said.

"He doesn't scare me," Alan Mendelsohn said. "I've read *Moby Dick*."

14

On the bus to West Kangaroo Park, we took turns reading a page at a time of the Mind Control course to each other. The first part was just like the lecture Samuel Klugarsh had given us. There was the picture of the light bulb, the cauliflower-brain, the radio diagram, the radio diagram-cauliflower-brain, and the guy looking happy who had taken the Klugarsh Mind Control course. The book was all in capitals, set far apart, with big spaces between the lines. It was mimeographed in fuzzy purple letters. On every page there was a slogan like the ones on the signs in Samuel Klugarsh's bookstore:

> THINK BEFORE YOU ACT
> BEFORE YOU THINK
> BEFORE YOU ACT.

Or:

> NEVER PUT OFF UNTIL TOMORROW
> WHAT YOU CAN DO YESTERDAY.

Even though there were a lot of pages in the book, there weren't many words, and the pages went by fairly fast. What with the big print, and the big spaces, and the slogans on every page, there wasn't much text. After we got through with the part that was just a repeat of Samuel Klugarsh's lecture, and all the pictures and diagrams, there were only a few pages left.

The section on how to use the Mind Control Omega Meter just said to clip the wires to your earlobes, and

59

make yourself comfortable, and try to produce omega waves. It said that when you start putting out omega waves, the machine would automatically play "Jingle Bells." We already knew all that. The book also told how to change batteries.

The last section was about how to control the thoughts and actions of others. It said that after you've had some practice with the Omega Meter—when you can produce omega waves with pretty good regularity—then all you have to do is look at a person who isn't concentrating on anything in particular, and say to the person, mentally, "My will is stronger than yours. You must obey. My will is stronger than yours. You must obey." Then you tell the person what you want him to do, mentally, and he does it.

The book said that after you get real good at controlling the thoughts and actions of others, you don't even have to look at them. You just think—and they do whatever you tell them. Then the promise that any person who has the power of Klugarsh Mind Control will never use his power to steal money or overthrow the government was printed in a little box—and we were through with the book. We weren't even halfway home.

Alan Mendelsohn sort of leafed back and forth through the Mind Control course. He didn't say anything, and neither did I, but we were both feeling sort of uneasy about the whole thing. "You don't think Samuel Klugarsh cheated us, do you?" I wanted to ask him, but I didn't. I didn't say anything.

Then we got the Omega Meter out. We looked it over. It was a transistor radio—the cheap kind—the kind they sell in drugstores around the bus station in Hogboro for three dollars and nineteen cents. There was some red-label tape over the name of the radio. It said OMEGA METER—FOR KLUGARSH MIND CONTROL STUDENTS ONLY. The volume sign and tuning knobs had big blobs of glue on them so you couldn't turn them, and a metal switch had been added—it stuck out of the middle of the radio. Two wires, about two feet long, came out of crude holes punched in the radio. They had clips on the ends.

Alan Mendelsohn flipped the switch. The Omega Meter buzzed. The two alligator clips accidentally touched and made a little yellow spark. He flipped the switch off.

"Do you think any of this is going to work?" I asked him.

"Of course it is," Alan Mendelsohn said. "Sure it works. I mean, we have twenty-four dollars invested in this setup. We ought to at least give it a real good try. It will work. Why shouldn't it work? Anyway, if it doesn't work, maybe we can find somebody to sell it to."

Alan put the Omega Meter and the Mind Control course back into the paper bag. Neither of us said anything for the rest of the ride. We got off the bus near Alan Mendelsohn's house. We decided to go there and practice with the Omega Meter. Nobody was home at Alan Mendelsohn's house. His father was at work and his mother had gone to her handwriting analysis class. She'd be gone for the rest of the afternoon. Alan made us each a peanut butter and banana sandwich and a glass of root beer, and we went into his room to work with the Omega Meter.

I tried it first. The alligator clips hurt, and after a while they made your earlobes all red. I tried to produce omega waves sitting, standing, and lying down. Nothing worked. The Omega Meter buzzed—my ears hurt—and no "Jingle Bells" played.

Then Alan Mendelsohn tried it. He sat down on the floor with his legs crossed. "This is called the lotus position," he said. "Swamis and yogis sit this way when they meditate."

Alan closed his eyes and breathed very deeply and noisily through his nose for a long time. "This is to make me calm," he said. Then he clipped the wires to his ears. The Omega Meter buzzed as it had for me. Alan Mendelsohn did not give up. He pressed his palms together and shut his eyes very tight. Beads of sweat started to appear on his forehead. Still the machine buzzed. He kept on meditating. The machine kept buzzing. After a while, he was meditating so hard that his hands were shaking. Still the machine buzzed.

"Let me try it again," I said.

"You might as well," Alan Mendelsohn said. "I'm getting tired, and my ears hurt."

We had another root beer before I took my turn. I was sort of impressed by Alan's meditating, and I decided I would try it too. I got a pillow from Alan's bed and sat cross-legged on it. I pressed my palms together and did deep breathing until I felt sort of dizzy. Then I clipped the wires to my ears and switched the machine on. It buzzed. I wasn't able to keep it up as long as Mendelsohn had. My back started to hurt as well as my ears.

"I want to try again," Alan Mendelsohn said. "This time I'm going to chant 'Om.' " Alan has this book, *Advanced Lessons in Yoga and Meditation*—that's where he learned all about the lotus position and chanting "Om."

"Ommmmmmmm," he hummed. "Ommmmmmmm, Ommmmmmmm, Ommmmmm, Ommmmmmmmmm." It sounded sort of nice. "Chant with me to help me get in the mood," he said.

"Ommmmmmmmm," I hummed.

Alan clipped the wires to his ears.

"Ommmmmmmmmm," he chanted.

"Ommmmmmmmmm," I chanted.

He flipped the switch. *Bzzzzzzzz* went the Omega Meter.

We kept it up for as long as we could. Then we switched off the machine and looked at each other.

"Maybe there's something wrong with the machine," I said.

"We should have had it tested when we were at Samuel Klugarsh's bookstore," Alan Mendelsohn said.

"I have to go home soon," I said. "What do you think we should do with this machine?"

"Maybe we can return it to Samuel Klugarsh," Alan Mendelsohn said.

"Do you think he might give us our money back?"

"Maybe he'll let us trade it for books."

"Well, I'm going home," I said, not moving.

"Yeah, well, Leonard, see you tomorrow," Alan Mendelsohn said, not moving.

"Yeah, well."

"Yeah."

"Damn it, this machine is a fake," I said. "We got gypped. We wasted all our money that we were going to buy used comics and weird books with. What made you think that this would work? It's all your fault. I would never have bought this thing if you didn't want to." I was pretty mad at Mendelsohn all of a sudden.

"It wasn't my fault," Mendelsohn said. "You never said that you had any doubts. If you didn't want to spend your money on this, you should have said something."

"I guess we both got gypped," I said.

"I guess we did."

We both sat still for a long time. Neither one of us said anything. Then we both started to laugh. Alan Mendelsohn pushed me. I was still sitting in the lotus position, and I fell over on my back, my crossed legs in the air. I started laughing so hard that I couldn't get up or uncross my legs. "Klugarsh Mind Control," I howled, "Klugarsh, Klugarsh, Klugarsh!"

"I am Klugarsh, famous scientist and genius," Alan Mendelsohn said. "See this picture of a light bulb? See this picture of a silly idiot smiling? I can talk to people on Mars. Klugarsh Research Associates has developed this cheap transistor radio that talks to Mars."

I was laughing so hard that my eyes were wet with tears. Alan Mendelsohn was really funny.

"See, I clip these things to my ears, and throw the switch, and produce omega waves—then I talk to Mars," Alan Mendelsohn said. He clipped the wires of the Omega Meter to his ears and threw the switch. The machine buzzed. "Now I'm in the office of the Martian High Commissioner, drinking fleegix," Alan Mendelsohn said. Then he began to laugh so hard that he couldn't talk. Both of us were flat on our backs, laughing, with tears running down the sides of our faces and into our ears. The Omega Meter attached to Alan Mendelsohn's ears buzzed away. We laughed and laughed until it hurt to laugh any more. Then we just lay there sighing. The Omega Meter buzzed.

"We're really suckers," Alan Mendelsohn said. "I'm supposed to be smart, but Samuel Klugarsh really made a monkey out of me." He was still sort of chuckling. "I give up."

We both lay there, getting over having laughed so much. We lay on the floor listening to the Omega Meter buzz. Alan Mendelsohn was apparently too weak from laughing to shut it off. For a long time we listened to it buzz. Then it stopped buzzing, and a set of silvery chimes played "Jingle Bells."

15

We were amazed, to say the least. The Omega Meter played "Jingle Bells," beautifully, almost all the way through. Then it started buzzing again, played a few more notes of "Jingle Bells," and went back to buzzing. Alan Mendelsohn and I stared at each other.

"How did you do that?" I asked him.

"I really don't know," Alan Mendelsohn said. "I was just lying there—sort of knocked out—and it played 'Jingle Bells.'"

"But, in your head, how did you feel when it started playing?"

"I don't know—good, I guess. I felt sort of good."

"Good? How good? Can you remember what you were thinking?" I asked.

"I wasn't really thinking anything. We were just lying there, remember? We were all tired out from laughing so much. I was lying here like this. I wasn't thinking. I felt tired and sort of good, and it started playing. I remember the last thing I said was 'I give up,' and . . ."

The machine started playing "Jingle Bells" again. It played it all the way through twice while we listened. Then it started buzzing again.

"Here, Leonard, you try it," Alan Mendelsohn said. "Put the wires on, and then sort of flop down and say, 'I give up.'"

I tried to remember the way we felt after all the laughing. I put the clips on my ears and flopped over backward. "I give up," I said. The machine played "Jingle Bells." I got it to play all the way through, and a little more, the very first time.

Then Mendelsohn wanted to try it again, and then I did. We traded it back and forth until my mother telephoned to ask if I was planning to ever come home for supper.

I left the Omega Meter at Alan Mendelsohn's house. He was supposed to come over to my house the next morning, and we'd practice together. I took the Mind Control course home with me to read over carefully, in case we'd missed anything—which didn't seem likely.

I got home. My father was waiting at the barbecue. It was starting to snow. Both my parents were sort of bugged about something. I could tell they wanted to talk to me. At the table it started.

"Leonard," my father said, "do you feel that Dr. Prince is helping you?"

"Sure," I said.

"Your mother is a little worried about his letting you take time off school like this," my father went on.

"It was his idea," I said. "I didn't want to take any days off—at first—but now I see that it was a good idea, and it's helping me make a better adjustment and become a better student."

"I don't see how taking days off school can make you a better student," my mother said. "You know I tried to call Dr. Prince on the telephone today, and he wouldn't talk to me. He said it would compromise his confidentiality if he spoke to me, and all he would say was that if I wanted a doctor of my own, he'd be happy to refer me to one. Why should he think I need to see a psychologist? Leonard, what sort of things have you been telling Dr. Prince about me—about us?"

I could see I was going to have to be careful with this. It was a lucky thing I had read that book about psychiatry. "I've been telling him that you're worried about me because I don't do well in school—and that upsets me and makes me worry about you, and that makes it even harder for me to do my schoolwork. I guess maybe Dr. Prince thought that you were so upset about me that you needed someone to talk to—I mean, you called him, didn't you?"

"Leonard, you don't have to worry about me," my mother said. "It's very kind of you, but I want you to concentrate on working with Dr. Prince and bringing your grades up. You're sure he's helping you?"

"Oh, yes," I said. "I'm not feeling nervous anymore, and I really feel sure that when I go back to school things are going to be very different."

"Well, that's all we wanted to know, son," my father said, "Would you like another piece of barbecued chicken?"

After supper I went to my room to study the Mind Control course. I lit up a cigar and started the book at page one. The only thing I hadn't really paid much attention to was the little slogan on every page. They seemed sort of sappy at first glance. I tried to figure out if maybe they contained some message I had missed the first time. They still seemed sort of sappy. For example:

> FEELINGS ARE FACTS.
> IF YOU FEEL A THING IS SO—
> IT IS!

And:

> DAMN THE TORPEDOES,
> GRIDLEY—
> FULL SPEED AHEAD!

And:

> NEVER TRY
> TO REASON WITH FEELINGS—
> OBEY THEM!

I really couldn't make much sense out of the slogans. Finally, I put the book away and tried to practice my omega waves without the meter.

The practice paid off. When Alan Mendelsohn brought the Omega Meter over the next morning, I found I could get it to play "Jingle Bells" for ten or fifteen minutes at a stretch. Alan had stayed up late practicing with the Omega Meter, and he could do even better, but he couldn't tell when he was producing omega waves without the meter, and I could. We took turns all morning, and by lunchtime, had gotten so we could turn the omega waves on and off.

My mother made lunch for us: noodle soup and grilled cheese sandwiches. After lunch she asked us to take Melvin for a walk. We put on our coats, leashed up old Melvin, and went outside. It was cold and crisp. Melvin liked that kind of weather, and he was almost wide awake. We sort of strolled around the neighborhood, and Melvin lifted his leg on various things.

"Have you noticed that Melvin sort of favors his right leg?" Alan Mendelsohn asked. "Let's try using Mind Control to get him to use his left leg." We came to one of Melvin's regular stops, a lamppost around the corner from my house. We both went into state twenty-six and mentally commanded him, "My will is stronger than yours. You must obey. My will is stronger than yours. You must obey. Lift your left leg." Melvin lifted his right leg as he usually did.

"This may not work on dogs," I said. "Let's find a human who doesn't seem to be concentrating on anything in particular. There wasn't a soul on the street. This was one of the things I had first noticed about West Kangaroo Park. There were never any people walking around. In the old neighborhood there were always people walking, people standing and talking, people just standing, people leaning out of their windows. You never saw anybody in the new neighborhood.

"Let's go where there are some stores," Alan Mendelsohn said.

There weren't any stores at all near our house—another difference from the old neighborhood, where you could walk down to the corner and get a Fudgsicle or a comic book. It was a walk of about three-quarters of a mile to the street where all the stores were. They weren't really stores, in the sense of stores being little places that sold things. They were more like shopping centers—little bunches of stores clustered around a parking lot, and big bunches of stores spread out along a big parking lot. You were supposed to drive to them—you weren't supposed to walk. In fact, there weren't any sidewalks, and Alan Mendelsohn and Melvin and I had to walk in the gutter with cars whizzing by.

There weren't even any people to be found on the big shopping street. Everybody was either in the stores or in their cars.

"Where are we going to find some people to practice on?" I asked.

"There!" Alan Mendelsohn said. He pointed to a gas station on the next corner. There were four or five guys standing around, drinking soda pop and leaning on the fenders of cars. "These guys aren't concentrating on anything in particular," Alan Mendelsohn said. "Let's give them a try."

"What shall we tell them to do?" I asked.

"Let's pick one—that guy in the hat. Let's tell him to take off the hat and scratch his stomach."

We went into state twenty-six. "My will is stronger than yours. You must obey. My will is stronger than yours. You must obey. Take off the hat and scratch your stomach." Nothing happened. We tried it again. Nothing. And again. Nothing.

"Maybe we need to practice the omega waves a little more," Alan Mendelsohn said.

"Maybe we do," I said. "Are you looking at the guy?"

"Looking right at him," Alan Mendelsohn said.

"Well, I can't think what we're doing wrong," I said. "Maybe he's thinking."

"He doesn't look as though he's thinking," Mendelsohn said.

"No, he sure doesn't," I said. "He doesn't look as though he ever had a thought in his life."

The man slowly took off his hat with his right hand, and with his left hand slowly scratched his stomach with a circular motion.

"It worked! It worked!" We jumped up and down.

"Tell him to bend over and bark like a dog," I said.

"Tell him to put his fingers in his ears," Alan Mendelsohn said.

"Tell him to dance," I shouted.

"Yes, tell him to dance!"

We went into state twenty-six. In a little while the guy in the hat was doing a private little dance, sort of a jig, shuffling his feet and bending his knees. When the other guys hanging around the gas station noticed the guy in the hat dancing, he looked sort of sheepish and embarrassed—as though he hadn't realized he was dancing—which, of course, he hadn't.

Alan Mendelsohn and I were hugging each other and dancing along with the guy in the hat.

"This thing has fabulous possibilities," Alan Mendelsohn said, "fabulous possibilities."

16

It turned out that the possibilities of Klugarsh Mind Control weren't as fabulous as Alan Mendelsohn had thought. For one thing, you needed to find someone who wasn't thinking anything in order to control them. People without a thought in their heads aren't as common as it would appear. Also, getting people to take off their hats or rub their bellies was about the best we could do. The guy in the gas station who did a little dance was our best subject all day.

We wandered around the shopping area of West Kangaroo Park, looking for subjects. The pickings were slim. We would do much better back at school—but we still had two more days of suspension/therapy and then the weekend before we could go back. Alan Mendelsohn had said he wondered how anyone could consider suspension from school as a punishment—especially suspension from a lousy school like Bat Masterson, but he was wishing we could be back. It's like this: As soon as you are locked out of a place and told that you can't come back in, you start thinking about getting back in. Even after we talked— even after we understood how it worked—we both would have been glad to get back into school a couple of days early.

We got cold looking for Mind Control subjects, and went back to my house. Melvin wasn't used to long walks, and he was exhausted. My mother was waiting for us to turn up.

"Alan, your mother has been calling. Your father is

leaving on a trip, and you're supposed to go right home and say good-bye to him," my mother said. "Leonard," she said to me, "the Old One called to say that her vacuum cleaner is broken. Tomorrow, will you take our vacuum cleaner to her apartment, pick up her broken vacuum cleaner, and take it to the repair shop?"

All this made sense. The Old One needs a vacuum cleaner every day because of the piles of sunflower seed shells and other debris that the parrot leaves around. Not to mention Grandfather. Before he left, I asked Alan Mendelsohn if he'd like to come with me to my grandparents' apartment in the old neighborhood. He said that sounded fine—he'd call me on the telephone that night. I looked forward to showing him around.

Alan Mendelsohn called that night, as he said he would. It seems his father had to go to New York City, where his company had its headquarters, all of a sudden. Alan said it was no big deal, but there was this sort of tradition in his family, where, when the father goes on a trip, everybody has to gather around while he gives them advice before he goes—things like don't forget to feed the cat, and always turn off the taps after you've finished using the water. Alan said it was all right for him to go with me on my vacuum-cleaner delivering errand the next day.

When we got to the old neighborhood, Alan Mendelsohn got really excited. "This is like The Bronx! This is like The Bronx!" he kept shouting as we rode down streets of brick four-story apartment houses. When we got off the bus to walk to the Old One's apartment, he said, "This even smells like The Bronx!" He really liked the old neighborhood. I knew he would.

We stopped and looked in the window of the fish store. All the fish were lying dead on the crushed ice, except some crabs who were feebly waving their claws around. It smelled good. It was a good fish store. Everything was fresh. There was seaweed packed between some of the fish. People in West Kangaroo Park must think that fish come out of the sea frozen and packed in little square boxes.

Alan Mendelsohn was excited. There had been a fish store in The Bronx. I was sure there had been. And there had been a bakery where they actually baked things, as opposed to having them delivered in white cardboard boxes from a truck at eight o'clock in the morning. The bakery not only smelled good, but you could buy broken cookies for a nickel. We got a dime's worth, still hot, and ate them out of a white paper bag with little stripes, and a grease spot from the cookies. It felt good to be in the old neighborhood. It must have felt even better to Mendelsohn because he had no way of knowing such things existed outside of The Bronx.

Another thing they have in the old neighborhood is cobblestones and trolley tracks. The trolley doesn't run anymore, but the tracks are still there—and a lot of the streets have these yellowish, squarish stones that you can turn your ankle on. They don't have them anywhere but the old neighborhood—and The Bronx, as I found out from Alan Mendelsohn.

If being in the old neighborhood made Alan Mendelsohn excited, being in the Old One's apartment made him almost crazy. "My grandmother has an apartment just like this!" he shouted. It turned out that his grandmother even had a parrot. He was beside himself. He ate up the goop made of ground-up soybeans and raisins and honey as though it was the best stuff he'd ever eaten. He played with the parrot, he made conversation with the Old One, who didn't really want to talk—she was concentrating on catching up on her vacuuming. Mendelsohn even wanted to see Uncle Boris's movies. That was a fatal mistake.—Once Uncle Boris started showing movies, they went on and on until people started to scream and thrash about. I went out with the broken vacuum cleaner while Uncle Boris and Alan Mendelsohn set up the screen.

When I got back from the repair shop, where the man

had said it would take eight months to fix the vacuum cleaner because they had to order parts from Romania, Alan Mendelsohn and Uncle Boris were talking and drinking tea out of glasses. They had already gotten through Uncle Boris's movie of the feet of everybody in the family, unto fourth and fifth cousins. Just the feet, you understand—no faces, no bodies—just feet. Also they had viewed Uncle Boris's zoological study of a squirrel in the park. This was a one-hour movie of a squirrel Uncle Boris liked—the squirrel running up a tree, the squirrel running from branch to branch, the squirrel sitting still, the squirrel eating a nut Uncle Boris had given it. It had taken me an hour and fifteen minutes to take the broken vacuum cleaner on the bus, drop it off at the repair shop, and come back.

"Hey, Old One," I shouted, "the man says it will take eight months to fix your vacuum cleaner!"

"I'm not surprised," the Old One answered. "They have to write to Romania to get parts."

I went into the dining room, where Uncle Boris and Alan Mendelsohn had set up their movie theater. They were talking about Samuel Klugarsh!

"Then I didn't see Klugarsh for some time," Uncle Boris was saying. "After the scandal over the Egyptian relics, he dropped out of sight, even though no one could prove he had any connection with the matter. Klugarsh reappeared some years later as a Chinese professor of mathematics named Yee Chi Poy. In that disguise he made some trips to Mexico, where he obtained a remarkable idol made of agate that had once belonged . . ."

"Excuse me," I said, "Is that *our* Samuel Klugarsh he's talking about?"

"Yes," Alan Mendelsohn said. "Uncle Boris has known Samuel Klugarsh off and on for twenty-five years. It seems that Klugarsh probably stole the basic principles of Mind Control, and a lot of other stuff, from an ancient brotherhood that had its headquarters in Mexico."

"That's right," Uncle Boris said. "The Order of the

Laughing Alligator—a very old mystical brotherhood, said to have originated in Tibet or India or California, or one of those places. What Alan describes as Mind Control is probably something Klugarsh picked up from the brothers of the Laughing Alligator when he visited them in Mexico."

"Uncle Boris, do you think Samuel Klugarsh swindled us, or what?" I asked.

"Well, that would be hard to say," Uncle Boris said. "Samuel Klugarsh has always been regarded by some as a swindler. I myself have always thought of him as someone who sells people things they don't really need for more money than they're worth. If that's your definition of a swindler, then he is one. Of course, Mind Control does work, doesn't it?"

"Well, we can make people take off their hats and rub their bellies when we give them a mental command—and one guy did a dance," I said.

"I can't say that what you're describing is my idea of fun," Uncle Boris said, "but you have powers now that you didn't have before—even if they're boring powers. It seems to me that Samuel Klugarsh sold you something that's worth a bit less than you paid. But since you're interested in such things, I may as well show you my magic gem—more of a crystal, actually."

Uncle Boris wandered off to his room, apparently to get something.

"What's going on?" I asked Alan Mendelsohn.

"Somehow the subject of Samuel Klugarsh came up," Alan Mendelsohn said. "I don't remember how—or, yes I do. Your Uncle Boris had a picture of his feet. Apparently Samuel Klugarsh is a fifth cousin, once removed, of Uncle Boris. Anyway, he mentioned Samuel Klugarsh, and I said, 'That's the guy we bought the Mind Control course from!' And your uncle wanted to know about that, and I told him. Then he started in on all this history about Samuel Klugarsh. It seems that Samuel Klugarsh has been involved in all sorts of shady deals. He was telling

me about it when you came in. Now he appears to have
gone to get some sort of magic gem. Do you know anything about that?"

I told Alan Mendelsohn that I had never heard anything about a magic gem. This was the first I had ever
heard about Uncle Boris having an interest in anything
other than his movie camera, feet, clouds, and squirrels.
Uncle Boris came back.

He had a little leather bag, tied at the top. "This is my
magic gem," he said. "I started to tell you about a Mexican
idol that Samuel Klugarsh brought back. Well, this was
one of the eyes of that idol." Uncle Boris produced a
dark green stone about the size of a marble, but not
quite round. It had flecks of brown and blue in it. It was
not clear, but looked like a little piece of earth that had
gone all hard and shiny.

"It doesn't look magic, but it is," Uncle Boris said. "It
is a sort of crystal—it vibrates at a certain frequency.
When certain people hold it—well, give it a try." He
handed me the stone. I felt it sort of wiggle in my hand.
He gave it to Alan Mendelsohn. As soon as he took it,
the stone began to give off a yellowish light.

17

"Well, well! My, my! Mercy, mercy!" Uncle Boris seemed to be very impressed by the fact that the magic gem had given off a yellow light when Alan Mendelsohn took hold of it.

"I never saw it do that before," Uncle Boris said. "It vibrates for certain people—that's supposed to show that you're psychically sensitive—but I never saw it light up before. You don't recall ever having heard anyone in your family mentioning that your ancestors came from a place called Mu? Lemuria? Anything like that?"

"The Ukraine?" Alan Mendelsohn asked. "That's where my great-grandfather came from."

"Mu and Lemuria and Atlantis are lost continents that are supposed to have existed a long time ago—and then sunk under the ocean. Samuel Klugarsh told me that this stone had originally come from some such place, and that it would light up if it were ever touched by a native of one of those lost continents. The thing about Klugarsh is that the stuff he sells is always real—but it isn't always what he says it is. He might sell you a real emerald, and tell you it was a rare Venusian green diamond. There's something special about this gem of mine, but I don't know if it really comes from Lemuria. For all I know it might come from the moon. Samuel Klugarsh used to have a brass potato that came from the moon—or so he said. At any rate, Leonard, your friend Alan Mendelsohn is a special sort of person, whether he's a Lemurian or not. The gem lit up like a little light bulb when he touched it, and it never did anything like that before."

Alan Mendelsohn was still holding the gem, and it was still giving off a definite yellow light.

On the bus back to West Kangaroo Park, we made a fellow take off his hat and rub his belly. We tried to make the same guy blink his eyes, stick his tongue out, and put his fingers in his ears—but all he did was take off his hat and rub his belly. We decided that Mind Control was boring, and that the next day we'd go back to Samuel Klugarsh's bookstore and try to get our twenty-four dollars back. What did we have to lose? We figured that even if he wouldn't return our money, maybe Samuel Klugarsh would let us trade the Omega Meter and the Mind Control course for something more interesting. I would have settled for one of those Lemurian gems—if it would light up for me the way it did for Alan Mendelsohn. We agreed to get up early and take the first bus into Hogboro. We were going to have breakfast at the Bermuda Triangle Chili Parlor.

18

It was just getting light—the sun wasn't up—when we got on the early bus for Hogboro. We had the Omega Meter and the Mind Control course in a brown paper bag. We had the leftover money we had not spent the last time we were in Hogboro, and a few additional dollars scraped from various secret savings. We had about twenty dollars between us.

It was quiet and sort of deserted around the bus terminal. A few people were sleeping on the waiting room benches, and an old guy was mopping the floor. The rush hour wouldn't get started for almost an hour. Most of the stores were closed. There were sheets of newspaper covering the sample drawings in the window of the tattoo shop. We walked toward the Bermuda Triangle Chili Parlor. It was cold—the sidewalk was a funny gray color in the early morning light, and it bounced cold up at us. A few pigeons, looking ruffled and sleepy, walked around on the pavement—trying to work up to the decision to fly. The wind whipped our ankles and up our trouser legs whenever we came to an intersection. Winter had arrived.

The windows of the Bermuda Triangle Chili Parlor were all steamy. We could smell coffee and hear cups and plates banging together. Through the steam we could see three—four—five yellow light bulbs. We went in.

The inside of the place smelled incredibly good. Fresh-baked corn muffins had just come out of the oven. I know what they smell like, because my mother gets these heat-'em-yourself frozen corn muffins that you make in the toaster. Even those smell all right—but this smell could only be the real thing. Besides, there they were, in a steaming pyramid on a big platter on the counter. We sat down on two stools, right in front of the corn muffins.

"Two corn muffins and two hot chocolates, am I right?" said the guy behind the counter. The hot chocolate was a great idea, and different from any I ever had before. I think it was made with milk instead of water. It was thick and foamy—and there was a marshmallow melting in the cup.

"Ah, the two scholars," a familiar voice said. It was Samuel Klugarsh. "Two corn muffins, heavy on the butter, and a hot chocolate with double marshmallows and whipped cream," he told the guy behind the counter.

"No eggs today, Mr. Klugarsh?" the counterman said.

"Not really hungry," said Samuel Klugarsh. "I had a late supper."

"We were going to come and see you after breakfast," Alan Mendelsohn said.

"See me now," Samuel Klugarsh said. "Bring your cups over to this table—have a refill of the hot chocolate, on me." Samuel Klugarsh gestured us toward one of the little black marble-topped tables in the place. He was wearing a red and white striped jacket with a pink shirt and a bright green bow tie. He had plaid trousers, and loafers made of bright orange-colored leather.

"You boys are working on interstellar telepathic communication, are you not?" Samuel Klugarsh asked.

"We bought a Mind Control course and an Omega Meter," Alan Mendelsohn said.

"Mind Control—of course," Samuel Klugarsh said. "I don't know what I was thinking of. Well, you can't expect results overnight. These powers don't come easily to humans—but I give you my solemn word, the machine *will* play 'Jingle Bells,' if you keep working at it."

"Oh, it plays 'Jingle Bells,' " I said. "It played 'Jingle Bells' the same day we got it from you."

"What?" Samuel Klugarsh looked very surprised. "I mean, of course it did. Klugarsh Mind Control is a scientifically designed course. It works. It always works. Maybe you'd like to write me a little letter saying how you're satisfied with your Omega Meter."

"Well, that's what we came to see you about," I said. "We really aren't satisfied. The Omega Meter works all right—it plays 'Jingle Bells,' and we followed the instructions and we can go into state twenty-six whenever we want to—but when we give mental commands, the only thing we can get people to do is take off their hats and rub their bellies, and once we got a guy to do a little dance."

"I don't believe you," Samuel Klugarsh said.

"No, really," Alan Mendelsohn said, "that's all we can get people to do. We read the book, and we've been practicing on people, on dogs, and that's all we can get anybody to do."

"That's all?" Samuel Klugarsh was pretty excited. "Show me. Show me right now."

We looked around for somebody who wasn't up to much mentally. There was a guy sitting at the counter, wearing one of those red hunting caps. He was pulling little pieces off a hard roll and popping them into his mouth. Then he'd spend a long time chewing each piece, all the time gazing at the coffee machine as though he were looking right through it and a hundred miles away.

"Watch that guy," we said. We both went into state twenty-six, and in a few seconds the guy was taking his hat off and rubbing his belly.

"Come with me," Samuel Klugarsh said. "I've got some machines in the bookstore that I want to use to test you guys. Put their stuff on my tab," he shouted to the counterman, and he hustled us out of the Bermuda Triangle Chili Parlor.

19

Samuel Klugarsh unlocked the door of his bookstore. He seemed to be really excited. "I've got a secret room in the back, where I keep all my really sophisticated instruments," he said. We walked past all the black boxes with wires and tubes and dials and switches, past the shelves of books on mystical subjects, to a locked door at the far end of the shop. Samuel Klugarsh unlocked the door, and we went into a small room. There was not much furniture in the room—a table and two or three folding chairs. There was something large covered with a sheet.

"I'll soon know for certain whether you're in state twenty-six," Samuel Klugarsh said. He whisked the sheet off what turned out to be the largest machine of all. It was painted in bright colors, mainly red. It sort of resembled a big refrigerator with a thing like a barber pole coming out the top of it. Written across the front of the refrigerator part of the machine was TEST YOUR BRAINPOWER in bright yellow letters about six inches high. The barber pole had a clear glass tube running up the outside. At the bottom it said Mental Midget; a little further up it said Sorta Stupid; a few inches higher it said Just About Normal; above that it said Smarty-pants; then it said Professor; then Wizard; then Genius; then Out of This World. Coming out of the front of the machine was a pair of heavy wires that were attached to something that looked like the stainless steel bowl that my father made salads in. The bowl had tubes and coils of wire coming out of the top. The whole thing had been sprayed with gold paint.

"This is the most advanced machine to test brain waves known to man," Samuel Klugarsh said. "It will take just a few minutes to warm up." Samuel Klugarsh threw a big switch. The machine hummed.

"This looks like one of those gadgets you see in carnivals," Alan Mendelsohn said.

"I know," Samuel Klugarsh said. "Isn't that incredible? The world's greatest expert on brain waves was a Tibetan lama and neurosurgeon, and when I met him he was operating an attraction in Atlantic City, New Jersey. He had designed and built this machine. I bought it from him and had it brought here. Out of This World corresponds to state twenty-six. When I put the Thought-Collector helmet on your heads, just do your Mind Control routine. A colored liquid will rise up that glass tube. If it gets as high as Out of This World, you will be the first humans to produce enough omega waves to be in state twenty-six. There was one person who did it while the machine was in Atlantic City—but he turned out to be a proven extraterrestrial."

"Can't you produce enough omega waves to be in state twenty-six?" I asked Samuel Klugarsh.

"Sadly, I cannot," Samuel Klugarsh said. "You see, when I was in the military, defending our country, I sustained a serious injury in the line of duty. As a result I have a silver plate in my skull, which creates an electromagnetic anomaly that prevents my participating in omega wave production. I'd appreciate it if this was kept confidential."

We promised we would never tell. Samuel Klugarsh said that the brain wave machine had warmed up enough, and would I be the first to be tested. I let him put the Thought-Collector helmet on my head. He told me to go into state twenty-six. I did. The brain wave machine made a whistling sound, and a column of red liquid rose in the tube past Mental Midget, Sorta Stupid, Just About

Normal, Smarty-pants, past Professor, Wizard, and Genius. It stopped just short of Out of This World, and sort of bobbed up and down.

"Fantastic!" Samuel Klugarsh said. "And do you mean to tell me that you got to be able to do this just by reading my Mind Control course and practicing with the Omega Meter?"

We told him that we had.

"Let's try this helmet on the other gentleman," Samuel Klugarsh said. He put the helmet onto Alan Mendelsohn's head, and the red liquid shot all the way to the top of the tube—even quicker than it had when I had been tested.

"Excuse me," Samuel Klugarsh said. "I'm a little overwhelmed—you see, this is the greatest moment in the mental history of man. I need to sit down for a minute." Samuel Klugarsh staggered over to one of the folding chairs and slumped down into it, looking sort of sick. He sat there for a while, shaking his head slowly from side to side. Finally he spoke. "I want to thank you. I want to thank you for making my life worthwhile—you see, I never knew if I was on the right track until now. Now I know that Klugarsh Mind Control not only works, but is the ultimate development in the history of progress. This is a great moment, but I don't want to forget that you are my clients, and that I am here to serve you. Now what was it that you wanted to talk to me about?"

We couldn't tell Samuel Klugarsh that we thought Mind Control was boring. Not after his great excitement. Not after finding out how important it was to him that we could reach state twenty-six. We couldn't tell him that we wanted our money back. Samuel Klugarsh was looking at us with this strange expression—it was a little like the way Melvin looks at Grandfather, sort of like he expected us to scratch behind his ears or give him a biscuit. He was waiting to hear what it was that we wanted to talk to him about.

Alan Mendelsohn spoke. "We . . . uh . . . we . . . we

wanted to know if we could trade in our Mind Control course and Omega Meter for a more advanced course."

That was quick thinking. There was no telling if the advanced course would be any better—but at least the boring Mind Control book and the Omega Meter would be off our hands.

"Of course you do," Samuel Klugarsh said. "I must have neglected to tell you about Klugarsh's trade-in policy. You can trade in any course or book you are dissatisfied with or, in your case, have gone completely beyond, for seventy-three percent of its current sale price, less a small handling charge, for any selected Klugarsh product or publication. Of course you want to trade in the Omega Meter—you gentlemen are ready for highly advanced work."

"Maybe we could sort of look around the store and pick out some books worth seventy-three percent of twenty-four dollars, minus a small handling charge," Alan Mendelsohn said.

"Oh, no, no, no," Samuel Klugarsh said. "Those books are not for talented people like you. Those books are for the—please pardon the expression—poor schnooks who go through life hoping that something will happen to them, like being able to achieve state twenty-six and make people take their hats off and rub their bellies at their command."

I couldn't imagine anyone going through life hoping to be able to make people take off their hats and rub their bellies.

"For people of real psychic prowess like yourselves, only the best, only Samuel Klugarsh publications and training devices are good enough. I will advise you. Now, what are your interests? Interstellar travel? Forecasting the future? Influencing inanimate objects? Reading the thoughts of others? Communing with lost civilizations—Mu, Atlantis, Lemuria?"

That rang a bell. Alan Mendelsohn and I both thought

of Uncle Boris's magic gem from the lost continent. "What do you have in the way of lost continents?" Alan Mendelsohn asked.

"Lost continents? Certainly," Samuel Klugarsh said. "What you are asking for is the Klugarsh Mind Control Associates advanced course in Hyperstellar Archaeology. This will equip you to find the everyday clues to the existence of civilizations no longer with us." Samuel Klugarsh rummaged around in the back of a drawer in a file cabinet. He came out with a thick dusty-looking stack of papers. It was held together with three of those brass fasteners that look like a nail, except they are flat—you push them through the papers you want to fasten together, and then the flat part spreads out into two flat parts, and you fold them back, and you've got your papers fastened.

"Excuse me, there's a misprint," Samuel Klugarsh said, and he wrote something on the cover of the sheaf of papers. Then he handed it to us. It had said *Basic Lessons in Hyperstellar Archaeology*, but Samuel Klugarsh had crossed out the word *Basic*, and written the word *Advanced* above it, so the cover now read *Advanced Lessons in Hyperstellar Archaeology*.

"This normally costs one hundred and seventy-five dollars," Samuel Klugarsh said. "But since you are my favorite students, and including your Mind Control course as a trade-in—by the way, I'm allowing you the full price, and we'll forget about the handling charge—this will only come to eighteen dollars and fifty cents—and that's less than it cost me to produce. Fair enough?"

20

"Mr. Klugarsh, exactly what is Hyperstellar Archaeology?" Alan Mendelsohn asked.

"You know what archaeology is, don't you?" Samuel Klugarsh asked him.

"Sure," Alan Mendelsohn said. "Archaeology is the scientific study of the life and culture of ancient peoples, through the excavation of ancient cities, relics, artifacts, etcetera." Alan Mendelsohn was great at definitions, because of all his word-power books.

"That's almost right," Samuel Klugarsh said. "Close enough for purposes of our discussion." Alan Mendelsohn looked bugged. "Now," Samuel Klugarsh said, "Hyperstellar Archaeology differs from ordinary archaeology in two ways. Firstly, it concerns itself with the study of lost civilizations, such as Atlantis, Mu, or Lemuria—and the lesser-known lost civilizations such as Waka-Waka, Nafsulia, and Shabomm. The second way in which Hyperstellar Archaeology differs from the regular kind is that instead of digging in the ground to find out about the ordinary life of these lost cultures, we look for clues to their existence in our everyday culture of the present. You see, in times past, beings from other planets came to Earth many times in order to study the activities of Earth life forms. Occasionally extraterrestrials took human form in order to study human activity without making anybody self-conscious. In some cases, the scholars from other planets left records, which Hyperstellar Archaeology decodes. I'll give you an easy example.—Nafsu Cola, which is about the third most popular soda pop in these parts, is made from an ancient formula salvaged from the lost city of Nafsulia. Walter C. Gull, the multimillionaire who developed Nafsu Cola, was a student of Hyperstellar Archaeology. He found the formula disguised in a coded document which appeared to be a list of outdated post office regulations. As a Hyperstellar Archaeologist, Gull instantly recognized the document as an encoding of Nafsulian material. He decoded it, decided to mix up a batch of the stuff, began to sell it, and the rest is history."

I had never tasted Nafsu Cola, although I knew that it existed. Every now and then you run across it in some out-of-the-way candy store, the sort of place that sells Moxie, and jelly beans by the scoop. I had no idea that it was the third most popular soft drink.

Samuel Klugarsh was talking. "Along with the course, I will include a copy of *Yojimbo's Japanese-English Dictionary*, vital for any student of Hyperstellar Archaeology, and one—no—two magic gems from the lost culture of Waka-Waka." He dug into the file cabinet and came up with two stones. They looked a lot like Uncle Boris's magic gem that had been the idol's eye.

"Those stones," I said, "they don't vibrate or light up or anything, do they?"

"Why bless your heart, boy, of course they do," Samuel Klugarsh said. "Of course, we don't have the sophisticated energy sources they had in ancient Waka-Waka, so I've had these converted. You just unscrew them in the middle, like this, and drop in a one-point-three volt, H-C type hearing aid battery. In good old Waka-Waka, all you had to do was expose the magic gem to the great laser energy source in the middle of Waka-Waka city, and they'd have power for a year—but you'll find out more about that when you study your course. Shall I wrap it up? Oh, by the way, you get a specially fitted, red manilla folder that holds the Hyperstellar Archaeology course, the magic gems, and *Yojimbo's Japanese-*

English Dictionary, vital to the study of H.A. What do you say?"

I knew this wasn't a good deal. Alan Mendelsohn knew this wasn't a good deal. Neither one of us could ever say why, but we gave Samuel Klugarsh our eighteen dollars and fifty cents, and our Omega Meter and our Klugarsh Mind Control course. Samuel Klugarsh put the H.A. course, the Japanese-English dictionary, and the two magic gems into a perfectly ordinary red manila folder, the kind with the red ribbon stapled to it that ties around. We hadn't even bothered to ask why the Japanese-English dictionary. We figured it would all become more or less clear as time went by. Another thing that Alan Mendelsohn and I were feeling—we were not finished with Samuel Klugarsh. We would never be finished with Samuel Klugarsh.

As we left the store, he called out after us, "Don't forget—when you're through with that course, you can trade it in. It's worth thirteen fifty towards your next purchase—and you can keep the dictionary and the magic gems!"

There were a lot of pages in the Hyperstellar Archaeology course and, unlike the Mind Control course, they were filled with tiny, smudgy, mimeographed typing. Alan Mendelsohn and I spent the whole weekend either at his house or mine, reading the H.A. course. We'd take turns reading to each other, or just take turns reading a chapter silently while the other guy slept, or had something to eat, or played with the dog. By Sunday night, we had gotten most of the thing read, but not necessarily understood. There were lots of confusing things in the course.

A thing we did a lot of while we were reading the H.A. course was play with the magic gems. On close inspection, they seemed to be made of plastic rather than some kind of stone, but they were nice just the same. They buzzed and jumped and vibrated in our hands, and sometimes they would flicker or light up. The H.A. course didn't say anything about them, and we didn't have much of an idea what they were about. They were pretty, though.

The other thing that didn't make sense for a while was *Yojimbo's Japanese-English Dictionary*. We couldn't figure out what that had to do with Hyperstellar Archaeology for the longest time. We did though—when we were almost to the end of the course—but that came later.

The course, which was really just a book, told how there were clues to the existence of ancient civilizations all around us. It gave a lot of examples. It said that certain words in modern languages are really Lemurian or Atlantean words. It said that Haya and Doon were the two most important Nafsulian gods, and when people meet in America and Australia and say "How're you doing?" they are actually repeating an ancient Nafsulian greeting.

The course also said that the native populations of North America and Australia both came from Nafsulia. It said that the potato was not a native crop to this planet, and that the people of Waka-Waka had introduced it when they migrated to Earth from their native planet of Haku-Hola.

The course was full of bits of information like that—but it didn't prove any of them. Alan Mendelsohn discussed whether anything in the course was true. It could have all been made up. The whole thing was written by a Professor Keith Brian Swerdlov of Miskatonic University. He could have been lying.

"I don't see where any of this is scientific," Alan Mendelsohn said. "Scientific means the theories in this book should be supported by experiments or tests that we can duplicate ourselves and see if they work. This book just says that kosher salami originally came from the planet Pluto with the people who colonized the ancient lost city of Shabomm. It doesn't say why we should think so, or even give us any idea whether Shabomm existed. As far as I can tell, the whole thing could be a fake."

Of course, we hadn't finished reading the course. It was before Sunday evening that we had these doubts. Still, we kept pushing on. We kept reading the thing. Even though it seemed to be one wild claim after another, for example—the book said that chickens were actually a degenerate form of an animal much smarter than humans, that had existed in Mu. It said that there are occasional throwback genius chickens about as intelligent as Einstein.

Then it would go on to something else equally weird, like saying that packaged chocolate pudding would turn into a deadly explosive if one easily obtainable ingredient were added. Naturally it didn't say what the easily obtainable ingredient was, and there were no cases of genius chickens as smart as Einstein listed, so someone could go and look them up.

It was a frustrating book. I would have quit plowing through the hard-to-read mimeographed typed pages if Alan Mendelsohn had said something—and I think if I had said something, he would have quit—but it had become one of those things that you finish because you *have* to finish it—because the other guy is going to finish it. It was a self-boring contest between Mendelsohn and me.

21

On Sunday evening the course got interesting. It got interesting when Alan Mendelsohn was taking his turn reading to me. He had just gotten through a long passage about how the custom of eating chopped liver is not of Earthly origin, but was picked up from interplanetary travelers by the residents of Atlantis. I must say the book was past the point of being boring, and had become totally ridiculous. Mendelsohn and I had laughed so much that we couldn't laugh any more; we just read on— reading the book because somehow we had made an unspoken pact to read our way through to the very end.

Mendelsohn had gotten through the part about chopped liver. Now he was into a section of Lemurian prophecies. It seems the Lemurian wise men had predicted the Civil War, the airplane, the automobile, sliced bread, Frisbees, and the Hong Kong flu. So what? Anybody can say he predicted anything. I could say that I predicted that men would go to the moon. Unless I had some proof that I said it a long time before anybody went there, or looked like they'd go there, it wouldn't mean a thing. Then Alan Mendelsohn got to the interesting part.

" 'Also,' he read, 'the Lemurian sages predicted that one day accounts of their deeds would be read by two boys named Alan Mendelsohn and Leonard Neeble.' " I thought he was just fooling around—making it up. His surprised expression and sort of sputtering, pointing, poking at the book, I took to be acting. Good acting, but not real—how could it be real? How could our names be in the book? Alan showed me. In the same smudgy little mimeographed typing, there they were, our names. How was this possible? Was it some trick of Samuel Klugarsh? We didn't put anything past him, but how would he have done it?

Samuel Klugarsh didn't know we were coming. We had run into him at the Bermuda Triangle Chili Parlor. He hadn't been out of our sight the whole time we'd been with him. In order to insert our names, he would have had to type the whole page on a mimeograph stencil, and then run it off, and insert it in the book. Alan Mendelsohn had worked on the school newspaper in The Bronx and had used a mimeograph machine. He said it would have taken at least fifteen minutes, if Samuel Klugarsh was a fast typist and mimeographist. Of course, if Samuel Klugarsh had known in some way that we would be coming back, he could have prepared the Hyperstellar Archaeology course with our names in it—but how could he know we'd be back in only a couple of days—and how could he know that we would want to trade in our Klugarsh Mind Control course and Omega Meter? What's more, neither of us could remember having told Samuel Klugarsh our names. He usually called us "Gentlemen."

If there was a trick in it somewhere, we couldn't figure it out. Of course, if it wasn't a trick—at least not a trick of Samuel Klugarsh—if it was a trick of the ancient Lemurian sages, then it put the whole book in a different light. Then it meant that all the stuff about the origins of eating chopped liver, and packaged chocolate pudding being a deadly explosive with one ingredient missing, and superintelligent chickens—it might all be true. We had been making jokes and playing a dumb game with a book that might be true!

Right after the book mentioned our names, it went on to something totally unrelated, which seemed to be the style of the thing. It went on to talk about how rubber automobile tires are actually living beings, and have feelings and memories and personalities. When they get flat, it means they're dead.

We were confused. First the book had gone on and on with all sorts of weird, unproven statements, one after another—with no rhyme or reason. Then it mentioned us both by name! Then it went back to strange little snippets of information.

Yojimbo's Japanese-English Dictionary was compiled by Clarence Yojimbo, a beloved Japanese scholar, who was actually a beloved Venusian scholar in disguise. Since Venusians live upward of three thousand years, Clarence Yojimbo had the opportunity to reside both in Lemuria in its Golden Age and, much later, in Japan 図 during the late Tokugawa period. Yojimbo compiled a much-respected Japanese-English dictionary for the use of merchants doing business in Yokohama. What is singular about the dictionary is that when read backwards, noting only the second word in English in each entry, it is found to contain another book—a key to ancient Lemurian Mind Control methods, rediscovered briefly, and then lost again by the Order of the Laughing Alligator, of which Yojimbo was a member.

We got the Japanese-English dictionary out of the red manila folder. We turned to the last entry.

zū-zū-shii [zu´u-] 図々しい Impudent; audacious; bold; cheeky; saucy; unblushing; shameless; brazen-faced; lost to a sense of shame.

So the second word in English was *audacious*. The next to last entry in the dictionary was *zuzuki*, meaning *pushing one's opponent on the chest with one's head*.

The second word in the English part was *one's*, but it was misprinted with no apostrophe. So far we had "audacious ones . . ." We went up the page, writing down the second English word in each entry. Soon it began to make a sentence—then two:

> *Audacious ones push straight to the center. In order to advance mental power show caution and courage daring and patience.*

It made sense. We didn't understand it, but it made sense. We read on. Alan Mendelsohn read aloud—reading the second word in English from each entry, going from the back of the book to the front. It made sentences all right—but they were very hard to understand. Obscure, Alan Mendelsohn said.

> *A short song effortless. A single monorail charged with coal syrup. The metalworker's steel prospect imparts a candid lump of airworthiness to the short dandelion. Mark a post an object with wood screws of tacit approval. Aim silent mental wooden drum at Buddhist temple. Win (lose) by ten crosses. Profit net proceeds of one thousand yen. Turn a book upside down.*

Most of the sentences seemed to us to be saying something, but we couldn't figure out what. Sometimes it was a little easier:

> *To send thoughts mentally without speaking directly by special means telegraphically radio telegraphy it is best to use made of metal an antenna a fence a gate a sword a thing silver copper steel. To receive same similar procedure good.*

That seemed to us to be fairly clear. It was saying that to send or receive thoughts, like radio waves, you need an antenna.

We went through the dictionary slowly, backwards, writing down a word at a time, and puzzling over the groups of words, trying to see them as sentences. It was slow work. We hadn't covered very much of the dictionary by the time Alan's mother called on the telephone and said for him to come home at once.

Alan asked me if I'd mind if he took the dictionary home with him. He said he would stay up late and copy out some more stuff, and maybe recopy the parts that made sense into a notebook. I told him to go ahead. We'd talk about it more in school, the next day.

22

At school, the next day, Alan Mendelsohn had a notebook with a bunch of words copied backwards out of *Yojimbo's Japanese-English Dictionary* in it. He hadn't had time to organize them into sentences—he just copied as many as he could before going to sleep. We met before school to discuss our Mind Control program for the day.

I had a metal ruler. We tried it out as an antenna. There was some debate at first as to where it would be best to put the antenna. Alan Mendelsohn thought that it would work best if it were attached to the head in some way, held in the teeth, or balanced on top of the head, or maybe just Scotch-taped to the head. I thought it would work best if it was hand-held and maybe pointed at the subject. We tried it my way. It worked. Soon, just about every kid in the school yard had been zapped with a mental command. One by one, they removed their hats, if any, and rubbed their bellies, and in some cases, danced. All I had to do was point at the kid in question with the ruler, think my command, and off they'd go, uncapping, rubbing, and dancing.

Alan Mendelsohn and I were delighted. *Yojimbo's Japanese-English Dictionary* was definitely a source of good advice. We had enough time before the bell to try to figure out some more sentences from Alan Mendelsohn's notebook. He had copied the words in neat columns on the left-hand side of each page. He had about ten pages of words. We went down the column, pointing with a pencil:

Cost expenditure outlay employment casual hired (in the air)

We included parenthetical expressions as one word.

(brown-eared) chicken rich lovers conditions. Petition the Emperor. Conceal pyramid mark object thus (decide upon a matter) hand a definite answer. Interesting framework construction (be imposing in appearance).

None of this made any sense to us. It was too obscure, as Alan Mendelsohn liked to say. Then we came to some clearer parts.

Best way get results. Have mental picture illustration sketch example before requesting order to send to transmit to give an order. Execute an order. Do one's bidding. First see it, then send it.

We thought that over. I pointed the ruler at a kid, closed my eyes and tried to see the kid walking with his arms stretched out to the sides, putting one foot directly in front of the other, sort of waving his arms up and down, first one, then the other—a picture of a kid walking a tightrope. I gave the mental command. I opened my eyes. The kid was doing a perfect imitation of a tightrope walker. It was beautiful.

Alan Mendelsohn wanted to try it. He had something special in mind. He picked out a kid, pointed the ruler at him and closed his eyes. He opened his eyes, the kid stepped on his own foot, made circles in the air with his arms, and collapsed forward in a shower of schoolbooks, pencils, blue-lined three-hole notebook paper, and the contents of his lunch bag.

"This is it," Alan Mendelsohn said. "The ultimate trip. The Remote-control Trip. This is the culmination of my career as a tripper. This will be my masterpiece. Leonard, let me borrow the metal ruler until lunchtime"—there was still time before the bell rang to start school. I told Alan sure—he could borrow the ruler. The bell rang and we went to our classes.

I wondered what it would be like, coming back to school after all those days off. It wasn't like anything. Nobody paid any special attention to me. It was evident that nobody had noticed I hadn't been there.

The next bell rang. "Take your seats and get ready for the P.A. announcements," Miss Steele said.

I unscrewed the top of my ball-point pen and took out the little brass refill. I pointed it at Miss Steele. I closed my eyes and got hold of a mental picture. Then I gave the command and opened my eyes. Miss Steele was looking very uncomfortable. I had picked a tricky mental picture, but apparently it worked—I had imagined a smoker going crazy for a cigarette. I had seen Miss Steele lighting up outside the building on the way to her car, and I figured she had a pretty serious habit. She was starting to sweat. Finally she said, "I'll be gone for just a moment—Robert Robinson, will you please take charge of the class while I'm gone?" She left. I made a mental note to quit fooling with cigars before I got hooked.

Robert Robinson was perhaps the most obnoxious kid in the school. He was big and had muscles, and wavy hair, and no pimples, and was handsome in a sort of simpy way. He spent all his time looking at the backs of his hands, or combing his hair, or making his muscles twitch. He was Mr. Jerris's favorite kid. He could climb those ropes just like a cockroach.

I pointed the ball-point refill at him. It was working out just fine as a short-range antenna. I worked up a better mental image for Robert Robinson than I had for Miss Steele—it was someone who has to go to the bathroom but can't leave the place he's been assigned to stay. This was perfect for Robinson. Ordinarily, he would be clowning, and sort of looking handsome for the girls, and doing cool things like putting one foot on the front desk in a row, and sort of leaning forward and twitching his muscles. Now he had to concentrate on not wetting his pants, and that made it impossible to be funny or act cool, or crack jokes, or do much of anything but shift from foot to foot, and try, unsuccessfully, to look casual while doing it.

I had seen a detective program on television in which the crime had been solved on the basis of the fact that the detective knew that it takes seven and a half minutes to smoke a cigarette. Miss Steele was not going to come back without smoking her cigarette all the way down. The class was going wild, and Robert Robinson had nothing to do but rock from foot to foot and try to hold on. He was too dumb to simply walk out of the classroom, go to the bathroom, and come back in the hope that Miss Steele wouldn't have come back before him. Even if she had, he could have just told her that he had an emergency—or if he was too shy to say that, he could say he went out to look for her, or anything. But he was too dumb. She had told him to stay, and he just stayed—like a trained dog.

The P.A. started up. Mr. Winter said, "GOOD MORN ——WHEN THE SURF'S UP IN OLD CALIFORNIA, THERE'S JUST OLD PAINT AND ME; JUST A BOY AND HIS HORSE ON A SURFBOARD, WHERE THE WIND AND THE WAVES ARE FREE. SURFIN', SURFIN', SURFIN' WITH MY HORSE; SURFIN', SURFIN' WITH MY HORSE, DOO WAH, DOO WAH." He was singing. This was obviously Alan Mendelsohn's work. I waited until Mr. Winter finished his song. He was sort of sputtering around, trying to make sense out of what he had just done. I pointed my ballpoint refill at the loudspeaker. I made a mental image of a sound— that was obviously how Mendelsohn had done it.

"I WILL NOW GIVE THE CORRECT TIME," Mr. Winter said, "CUCKOO—CUCKOO—CUCKOO—CUCKOO—CUCKOO—CUCKOO—CUCKOO—CUCKOO—CUCKOO." The whole school was laughing. This didn't make things any easier for Robert Robinson.

There was a loud click. Mr. Winter had switched off the P.A. Miss Steele came back into the room. Robert Robinson ran out without a word as soon as he saw her. It took her until the bell rang to get things quieted down.

At lunchtime, Alan Mendelsohn and I met for a discussion of strategy. We agreed to cool it for the rest of the day. We had done so much Mind Controlling that we were getting dizzy. Also, we didn't want to create a full-scale riot like the time Alan had told everyone that he was a Martian. Between the opening bell of the day and the start of lunch period, we had caused people to be rooted to the spot, bark like dogs, have uncontrollable urges to do various things that they simply couldn't do with people watching. We had done a lot of tripping and a good deal of making people think that a notebook or a pencil weighed a hundred pounds. The whole school was like a circus, and we were the audience.

But it wasn't as much fun as we thought it would be. For one thing, part of the fun of the circus is the big crowd of people you're watching it with—that's why circuses are no good on television. With only Alan and me in on the joke, it wasn't all that entertaining to get people to do funny things. Also, those kids who weren't too stupid to realize that something strange was going on were getting scared. A couple of kids had even cried when Mr. Winter was cuckooing. People get scared when they think other people are going crazy.

We had decided to cool it. We wouldn't do any more tricks on people that day—and we would plan something really big for our new power. There was another sen-

tence Alan Mendelsohn had found in the dictionary the
night before:

> *To control minds (of) other people is good trick,*
> *but to control objects is great trick. Can a stone*
> *fly?*

We picked up a small pebble and went to work on it. It
didn't budge. We tried again and got it to move, so
slightly that we couldn't be sure it had moved. It took the
rest of the lunch period to move it an inch.

23

We had agreed to knock off Mind Control tricks for the rest of the day—at least big tricks that might get people stirred up. I did manage to knock twenty-two minutes off the school day by speeding up the master clock that controlled all the clocks in the classrooms. As we were leaving school, it occurred to me that everybody was going to be twenty-two minutes late in the morning. Except Mendelsohn and me. Later, Alan Mendelsohn persuaded me that we'd better be late too, so as not to arouse suspicion.

Alan Mendelsohn had a lot of junk in his room. He liked to pick up all sorts of things in the street and in empty lots. He had lots of wire and odd pieces of metal that came off cars and machinery. We headed for his house to see if we could work out a better type of antenna. On the way there, we picked up a brick from a place where they were building a house. That was going to be our test Mind Control subject. The idea was to try the different antennas on the brick—giving it the same mental command each time. The best antenna would get the best performance.

We set the brick in the middle of the floor of Alan Mendelsohn's room. Then we took turns giving it commands to rise into the air—without using any antenna at all. It didn't budge. Then we both commanded it at once. No results. Then we pointed the metal ruler and the ball-point pen refill at it and gave simultaneous commands. No soap. Alan got a big coil spring. He put that against his forehead and commanded the brick to rise. It wobbled a little. We tried loops of wire, half an army bayonet, a metal tennis racquet, a boy scout trumpet, and various odd bits of metal—we didn't know what they were. Nothing made the brick rise or do anything more than vibrate slightly, the way it might if a heavy truck went by.

Mendelsohn dug around in his closet, which was very full of all sorts of odd junk, and came up with something that looked really promising. It was a rabbit-ears television antenna, but not the ordinary kind. This one had knobs on it and eight rusty brass-plated hoops encircling the base, in addition to the two rabbit ears, each of which had a little crystal cylinder about halfway up with a coil of copper wire inside. Super Signal Booster it said on the plastic base in letters of tarnished gold. This definitely looked like it would do the job.

There were two wires coming out of the base of the Super Signal Booster, and we each took one of them and pressed the little brass horseshoes at the end to our foreheads. We gave the command, "Rise, rise!" The brick shot up to the ceiling and made a large dent.

Alan Mendelsohn and I looked at each other. This antenna really worked. We tried again. "Rise slowly!" The brick floated up to the ceiling like a balloon, and bounced gently against it. "Descend!" We forgot to say slowly. The brick fell—like a brick—and made another big dent in Alan's floor.

"We need to practice with this," Alan Mendelsohn said.

"This antenna certainly has possibilities," I said.

"With this antenna and a little practice," Alan Mendelsohn said, "we could . . ." his voice trailed off.

"We could make the school float," I said.

"Yes, we could!" Alan Mendelsohn said. "We could levitate it!"

"Levitate?"

"Yes, that's what it's called when you cause something

to float in the air. That's what we just did with this brick. It's just about the hardest thing to do in all magic. You almost never see it."

Alan Mendelsohn was really excited at the prospect of making Bat Masterson Junior High School float in the air.

"You don't think we could make it float away altogether?" I asked.

"We'd have to practice a lot first," Alan Mendelsohn said. "Just getting it off the ground is going to be no easy feat. What's more, we have to decide if we want to send it up empty or with everybody on board. If we send the school up loaded, we have to be very sure we can set it down again gently, or we'll wind up killing everybody."

Alan Mendelsohn had a point—in fact he had a number of them. Mind Control was one thing when you were dealing with a pebble, or even a brick—but when you started sending buildings up into the air, you had to know what you were doing. We needed to do a lot of practicing if we were going to get it right.

The workmen at the construction site had gone home. We went back to practice lifting bricks. Behind the place where they were building, there was a grassy hill. We went there and sat down with the Super Signal Booster pointing at the big square pile of bricks. The brick pile was forty bricks long and twelve bricks across; it was twenty bricks high. So there were four hundred eighty bricks to a level and a total of nine thousand six hundred bricks in the pile.

We commanded one brick to rise—just an inch—we didn't want to attract any attention. It rose up an inch, and then we commanded it to set itself down. Then we had two bricks rise an inch and set down again. That worked. Three bricks. Four bricks. Five. Six. Seven. Ten. Fifteen. Twenty. Twenty-five—and the twenty-five bricks dropped with a loud crash, landing slightly out of line, instead of settling neatly into rows as they had when we tried the same trick with a smaller number of bricks. A couple of the bricks even cracked when they fell.

"I was afraid of that," Alan Mendelsohn said. "We don't have enough power."

Just then an exterminator's truck came past. DR. KILZUM it said on the side of the truck, ALL HIS PATIENTS DIE. There was a picture of a cartoon guy in a doctor's suit. He had a bag full of carpenter's tools and was holding a Flit gun. For some reason I thought of Dr. Prince.

"Holy cow!" I said, "I've got an appointment in Hogboro with my psychologist in less than half an hour. I'm going to be late for sure."

"I'll ride into Hogboro with you," Alan Mendelsohn said. "I've got nothing to do."

We ran for the bus. We were lucky. One was just coming when we got to the bus stop. If we ran from the bus terminal to the office building, I'd only be late five minutes, or a little more.

We were sweating when we arrived at the building where Dr. Prince had his office. Alan rode up in the elevator with me. People stared at us—I guess we looked strange to them, two sweating kids in tennis shoes in a fancy office building in downtown Hogboro.

"Doctor Prince, this is my friend Alan Mendelsohn. Is it OK if he waits here for me?" I asked.

"Of course it's all right," Dr. Prince said. "You're more than five minutes late. You must be full of aggression. That's a good sign. Come in, Leonard, my boy."

I went into Dr. Prince's office. He seemed very happy that I had come in late. Psychologists are strange people.

"Well, Leonard," Dr. Prince said, "tell me what happened when you came back to school after being absent for four days."

"Nothing happened," I said.

"Nothing! See? What did I tell you?" Dr. Prince seemed really happy. I guess he was a nice guy—just misguided. "And you came here late," he went on. "You weren't afraid to be late. I'm really pleased with your progress, Leonard."

I decided to tell Dr. Prince about Klugarsh Mind Control, and Hyperstellar Archaeology, and making bricks rise into the air. He seemed to want so much for me to confide in him—it wasn't his fault that he was a psychologist and got things mixed up. I told him about going to Samuel Klugarsh's bookstore and everything that happened since. He made a note in his little book when I told him about the fresh corn muffins at the Bermuda Triangle Chili Parlor, and he wanted to know the address.

When I got through telling Dr. Prince all about my new powers, he said, "Leonard, I can't tell you how pleased I am that you trust me enough to share your psychotic fantasies with me. Now we'll really make some progress."

"They're not psychotic fantasies," I said, "I'm telling you the truth."

"You'll have to prove that to me," Dr. Prince said, rubbing his belly and removing an imaginary hat.

I had left my metal ruler and ball-point pen at Alan Mendelsohn's house, and we had hidden the Super Signal Booster in the bushes when we ran for the Hogboro bus. So all I could have done to prove my powers would have been to make Dr. Prince rub his belly and remove his hat—which he was already doing. Besides, I didn't really feel like proving anything to him. I was sort of mad at him for making fun of me. Let him believe whatever he wanted to.

24

Dr. Prince walked me to the door of his office. Alan Mendelsohn was sitting in the waiting room, reading a copy of *Psychology Today*. On the cover was a picture of the Mad Hatter from *Alice in Wonderland,* and written across the cover, diagonally, in yellow block letters, it said, HOW TO TELL IF YOU HALLUCINATE.

"I'm glad to see you're making friends, Leonard," Dr. Prince said. Alan Mendelsohn put down his magazine, and we both moved toward the outer door. Dr. Prince followed us. "Don't worry about a thing," he shouted down the hall as we headed for the elevator, "I've cured people twice as crazy as you!"

Alan and I rode down in the elevator. The people in business suits and high heels all looked at us again. The elevator filled up. "So the doctor says there's no hope for you?" Alan Mendelsohn asked me.

"No, he said it's incurable," I answered. The people in the elevator all looked at me. "The lucky thing is there isn't a leper law in this state, so I can live at home if I want to."

"Yeah, that's good," Alan Mendelsohn said, "otherwise you'd have to go to that place in Hawaii."

Somebody pushed the button, and the elevator emptied out on the seventh floor.

We were alone in the elevator. "Look," Alan Mendelsohn said, "have you got any money on you?" I had about four dollars. Mendelsohn had about six. "Let's have supper in the Bermuda Triangle Chili Parlor. I'll call my mother and tell her I'm eating at your house, and you can call home and say you're eating at mine. There shouldn't be any problem."

It was a good idea. We found telephone booths in the lobby of Dr. Prince's office building and made our calls.

The rush hour was almost over. The streets of downtown Hogboro were nearly empty. A few late workers rushed to catch buses and trains. The stores were closing. It was just about dark. Alan Mendelsohn and I set out for the Bermuda Triangle Chili Parlor, our Fargo Brothers Rum-Soaked Curley-Q's glowing red in the chilly wind.

As we got away from the downtown business district, the streets got quieter and emptier. We moved away from the warmth and bustle around the bus station and into colder darker streets. We zipped up our jackets and walked fast, puffing our cigars. A motorcycle club roared past us. KNIGHTS OF POWER it said on the backs of their jackets. Bunched together, the motorcycles made a noise like running a ruler along an iron fence or a radiator—only much louder. We watched the red tail-lights get smaller and smaller in the distance.

It was just a little bit scary. All the buildings around us were dark. They weren't office buildings. They contained little factories, tailor shops, wholesalers, and warehouses. They were all dark. There wasn't anyone on the street but us.

The lights of the Bermuda Triangle Chili Parlor, two blocks away, made a welcome sight. As we got closer, we saw that the storefront was surrounded by a little puddle of brightness made by the light bulbs behind the steamy window and the red neon sign which said EAT. Parked outside the Bermuda Triangle Chili Parlor were six or seven motorcycles—shiny ones, with all sorts of gadgets and decorations on them. Each of the motorcycles had a fancy dragon or alligator either painted in gold on the gas tank or worked into a fancy chrome backrest. We figured they belonged to the motorcycle club that had passed us earlier.

By this time, we could smell all sorts of good cooking smells and hear the faint clicking of dishes and silverware. When we opened the door, a blast of noise, warmth, and the most incredible smell of chili hit us. Now up to that time, my only experience with chili was stuff out of a can and stuff they served in the cafeteria in my old school. Right away, just from my first whiff, I could tell that this stuff was very different from the chili I had run across so far. When my glasses unfogged a little, I could see a sign hanging behind the counter. It said Chili—one dollar; Regular, H-Bomb, Green Death. The guy behind the counter was serving up the chili in white bowls. It seemed like everybody in the place was eating chili. The Knights of Power motorcycle club had pushed two tables together—they were eating the Green Death chili. I could tell because it was green. All the other chili was regular chili color.

"What's yours, boys?" the guy behind the counter asked. We played it safe and ordered the Regular chili. He handed us bowls of the stuff, a spoon apiece, and a stack of crackers, and we carried our stuff over to an empty table.

The chili tasted great. It was hot, too. Alan Mendelsohn said that he thought he could have handled at least the H-Bomb variety. I couldn't have—the Regular chili made me sweat and see little spots before my eyes. There was a sort of serve-yourself stainless steel sink, with racks of water glasses over it. You press the glass up against this metal horseshoe-thing with little rubber tips, and the glass fills up with cold water. We made quite a few trips to get water.

We liked the Bermuda Triangle Chili Parlor. It was warm and cozy and friendly. The motorcycle guys didn't seem sinister, or bad, or anything like that. They just ate their Green Death chili and talked quietly among themselves. In the kitchen, a radio was playing—some kind of foreign music I'd never heard before—it sounded like something between banjos and bells. It was nice.

Samuel Klugarsh walked in. He saw us and walked over. "Hello, students," he said. "Mind if I join you?" He went to the counter and came back with two bowls of Green Death. Then he went back to the counter again and returned with an enormous stack of crackers and a mug of hot chocolate with double marshmallows and whipped cream. I couldn't for the life of me figure out why this guy wasn't fat. Samuel Klugarsh crumbled the crackers into his two bowls of Green Death chili. "How are you doing with the Hyperstellar Archaeology?" he asked us.

One of the Knights of Power spun around and glowered at us for a moment. He had a big bushy mustache. Then he turned back to his friends and his chili. The motorcycle guy had distracted me. Samuel Klugarsh spoke again, "It was Hyperstellar Archaeology, wasn't it? Mu and Lemuria and Atlantis, and all that?"

"It's been very interesting, Mr. Klugarsh," Alan Mendelsohn said. "At first we couldn't understand the book at all—it just seemed to be full of all sorts of whacky facts. Then the Hyperstellar Archaeology course actually mentioned us by name."

"You're putting me on," Samuel Klugarsh said.

"No, no—it's the truth," I said. "The book said that the ancient Lemurian sages had predicted that one day two boys named Leonard Neeble and Alan Mendelsohn —that's us—would read an account of their deeds."

Samuel Klugarsh looked stunned. "Are you actually sure this happened?" he asked.

"It was right there in black and white, Mr. Klugarsh— actually blue and white, since it was mimeographed," Alan Mendelsohn said.

The biker with the bushy mustache—the one who had turned around and looked at us—was obviously listening in. He was leaning back in his chair so he could hear what we were saying. I never know what to do in situations like that—I mean, it's worse when you're the one listening and you can't help it. Sometimes people have family fights in restaurants, or holler at their kids, or talk about all kinds of personal stuff—and there you are, sitting right next to them. I didn't really care if the guy in the Knights of Power jacket listened or not, I decided. There was no way he was going to know what we were talking about anyway.

"If I hadn't actually seen proof that you guys could attain state twenty-six, I'd never believe this for a minute," Samuel Klugarsh said. "As it is, I have another copy of the course at my shop. I've never read it—that is to say, I've never read it for a long time—but I'll have a look at it. Where exactly did it mention you guys by name?"

"It was just before the part where it talks about *Yojimbo's Japanese-English Dictionary*," I said.

The motorcycle rider—the one who'd been eavesdropping—had a coughing fit. Samuel Klugarsh turned around and pounded him on the back. "What's the matter, buddy, did something go down the wrong way?" he said. "You've got to go slow with that Green Death if you're not used to it." He turned back to us. "Eating hot chili is an art," Samuel Klugarsh said. "The first thing you have to learn is to ignore the pain. You see, pain is your body's way of warning you that something is happening to it that is harmful—for example, if you put your finger in a candle flame, the pain tells you to take it out before it gets burned to a crisp. Now in the case of eating hot chili, the peppers give the illusion of pain. But in this case, it isn't harmful—there's nothing better for you than hot chili—so you just have to say to yourself that this isn't going to harm you." Samuel Klugarsh stopped talking to swallow a big spoonful of the Green Death. I could have sworn I saw blue sparks jumping when he dug into it. Then he covered his mouth with his fingertips and gave a modest burp.

Dr. Prince walked in. He was holding a slip of paper. I guessed it was the page from his notebook on which he had noted the address of the Bermuda Triangle Chili Parlor. His glasses were all fogged up.

"Look!" I said, "There's my psychologist!"

Dr. Prince had gotten into an argument with the guy behind the counter. It seems they only made corn muffins in the morning, and were usually all out of them by evening. Dr. Prince had come in for corn muffins, and corn muffins he wanted. He was giving the guy a hard time.

Dr. Prince saw us and came over. "Oh, hello, Leonard," he said. "I thought you told me this place had the best corn muffins in town. Now I come in here, and they won't sell me any. I'm most upset."

Samuel Klugarsh stood up. "Our young colleague is correct about the corn muffins," he said, "but he neglected to tell you that what this place is really famous for is the Green Death chili, a secret recipe of the owner. I advise you to try it. By the way, I am Professor Samuel Klugarsh, Fellow of the Royal Astromental Society." He shook hands with Dr. Prince and then took him by the arm to the counter. The two men came back to the table with a bowl of Green Death apiece. It was Klugarsh's third!

"Excuse me just for a moment," Samuel Klugarsh said, and returned to the counter.

"Ah, Leonard," Dr. Prince said, "you must excuse my perturbed state a moment ago. I become unreasonable when I am denied gratification I have been anticipating. This is your young friend . . ."

"Alan Mendelsohn," I supplied the name.

"Ah, yes, and is the other gentleman, Professor Klugarsh, the one you were telling me about? The one who sold you the course in Hyper . . . Hyper . . ."

"Hyperstellar Archaeology," Samuel Klugarsh said. He had returned to the table balancing four cups of hot chocolate with double marshmallows and whipped cream. Out of his pocket he took a great many saltines and deposited them on the table. "A fascinating topic, Hyperstellar Archaeology. We'll have a good old scientific discussion in a bit—but first, enjoy your meal, Doctor. I'm curious to know what you think of the Green Death chili."

Dr. Prince scooped up a big spoonful of the stuff. At first, after he had popped it into his mouth, he had a sort of musing expression; then he looked pleased; then he looked surprised; then he got very red; then he grabbed handfuls of saltines and stuffed them into his mouth—by this time he was sweating freely—then he ran to the stainless steel water dispenser and gulped three glasses of water. When he came back to the table, tears were streaming down his face. He loosened his collar and sat down. "Without a doubt, the best chili I've ever tasted," he said to Samuel Klugarsh.

Samuel Klugarsh leaned across the table and clapped Dr. Prince on the shoulder. "A gentleman and a scholar!" he said. "Now, eat up. If you don't go into shock from the first spoonful it's clear sailing after that. Eat up now. Then we'll have a good chat."

25

I was getting sort of angry at Dr. Prince. When I had told him all about Hyperstellar Archaeology and Lemurian Mind Control methods, he thought it was fantasy. Now, Samuel Klugarsh, who, by his own admission couldn't even attain state twenty-six, was telling him the same stuff, and Dr. Prince was listening politely—just because Samuel Klugarsh was an adult. It bugged me.

"And of greatest importance," Samuel Klugarsh was saying, "is *Yojimbo's Japanese-English Dictionary*, which is actually a secret key to . . . Tell Doctor Prince what *Yojimbo's Japanese-English Dictionary* is a secret key to, lads."

Alan Mendelsohn took up the story. "You see, *Yojimbo's Japanese-English Dictionary* was compiled by Clarence Yojimbo, who was not really Japanese, but a Venusian, who had lived a long time in Lemuria. If you read the book backwards, counting only the second word in English in each entry, it makes a book of instructions in ancient Lemurian Mind Control methods."

"And what are those?" Dr. Prince asked.

"Well, it tells you how to control people and then objects, with your thoughts. That's as far as Leonard and I have gotten. We're learning to move objects by mental commands. That's what Lemurian Mind Control is all about."

"That is utter nonsense!" someone said. It was the biker—the motorcycle guy who had been listening during our whole conversation. "In fact," he said, "I've never heard anyone get anything so utterly turned around. You're as wrong as you can be."

Samuel Klugarsh turned in his chair. "And what do you know of such matters, you ruffian?"

"I know a great deal about such matters," the biker said. "In fact, I probably know more about these things than any person alive."

"Sir," said Samuel Klugarsh, "you evidently do not know to whom you are speaking. I have devoted half my life to the study of the lost and obscure arts and sciences, the civilizations of the vanished continents—Mu, Atlantis, Lemuria, Waka-Waka, and so forth—and especially the study of hitherto concealed and unknown powers of the mind. My name is Professor Samuel Klugarsh."

"And my name," said the motorcyclist, "is Clarence Yojimbo."

There was a silence. Alan Mendelsohn and I stared at the biker. There was something strange about his appearance. It was nothing obvious, but somehow he didn't look like anyone we had ever seen before. His hair and skin were almost the same color, a sort of bronze color. He was very big, and there was something strange about his eyes. It was hard to pin down—he looked like an ordinary person, and he didn't.

"You'll have to prove that to me," Samuel Klugarsh finally said.

"You have sixteen dollars and forty-two cents in your pocket," the biker said. "Your underwear is blue with white stripes. There's a hole in your left sock, at the toe. In your refrigerator at home, there are six slices of garden variety pizza, which you intend to eat cold before you go to bed. The book you are reading every night in bed is called *Confessions of a Yugoslavian Streetcar Conductor;* you have gotten up to page 42. Tomorrow morning you plan to open your shop late, because you have to stop by the Motor Vehicle Bureau and pay a traffic fine for a ticket you got last April when you double-parked outside a doughnut shop. You own a cat named

Willy, who happens to have four ears. You found him in an alley in Durham, North Carolina, but you tell people he's a Martian spacecat. Is any of this information incorrect?"

Samuel Klugarsh really looked astounded. "No," he stammered, "every word you've said is absolutely correct."

"And, have you ever seen me before in your life?" the biker asked.

"Never," Samuel Klugarsh said.

The biker bowed from his chair to the Knights of Power motorcycle club, who had been listening to this whole exchange. The bikers burst into applause, whistling and cheering. Clarence Yojimbo gestured for them to stop. "Thank you, gentlemen, thank you."

"Wait a minute," Dr. Prince said. "All you have proven is that you are a remarkable mind reader. Not that I doubt your word—if you say you're Clarence Yojimbo, I have no reason to doubt you—but, surprising as your mental feats may be, they don't prove you are who you say you are."

"A reasonable objection," Clarence Yojimbo said. "I will now put your doubts completely to rest." He pointed to the pocket of his motorcycle jacket. Spelled out in little metal studs was the name Clarence.

"Bravo! Bravo!" shouted the Knights of Power.

"And now . . ." Clarence Yojimbo said, and with a flourish, pulled out and flipped open his wallet. In a little plastic window was a driver's license. "Note the name," he said, and passed the open wallet around. The license was made out in the name of Clarence Yojimbo.

"Brilliant! Brilliant!" said the motorcycle club.

"But are you *the* Clarence Yojimbo? The one we've been reading about?" Alan Mendelsohn asked.

"I am that most excellent person," Clarence Yojimbo said.

"Then . . . then you're a Venusian!" I said.

"Not so loud! Not so loud!" Clarence Yojimbo said.

"That's not something to shout about in a public restaurant."

"Shhhhh!" said the motorcycle club.

"Ordinarily, I'd never reveal myself like this," Clarence Yojimbo said. "The only reason I'm doing so is that I couldn't help overhearing your conversation—and you people have got everything so badly mixed up that I really had to take charge of the situation before you get into serious trouble. Besides, I've known that I was going to have to deal with these two boys since the old days in Lemuria."

"That's right!" Alan Mendelsohn said. "The book said that the ancient Lemurian sages predicted that Leonard and I were going to read about their deeds!"

"Read about them, and a good deal more," Clarence Yojimbo said. "But for now, let me clear up a few things. First of all, I will introduce my companions." He gestured to the motorcyclists, who had turned their attention to their bowls of Green Death chili again. "These good men are the last surviving members of the ancient Order of the Laughing Alligator. For the past few thousand years, that brotherhood has guarded the extraterrestrial secrets which all of you seem so interested in. These last surviving brothers—none of them under eight hundred years old—have been my constant companions and friends for the past few centuries." The Laughing Alligator brothers looked up from their chili and winked at us.

"Now, let's correct a few things," Clarence Yojimbo said. "Professor Klugarsh, the Hyperstellar Archaeology course was sold to you by an individual named Rodni Rubenstein, am I not correct?"

"Well, yes," Samuel Klugarsh said. "Ordinarily, I do my own research, but in this case . . ."

At this point, it suddenly started to sink in that we were sitting around talking to a Venusian. I felt the hair on the back of my neck stand up. My skin felt all tingly. I guess the Bermuda Triangle Chili Parlor, the Green Death chili, and everything were so unfamiliar that the addition of a supposed Venusian didn't really stand out as something exceptional right away. It seemed that the situation had crept up on everyone in the same way, because Dr. Prince was listening quietly, smoking his pipe, while Samuel Klugarsh and Clarence Yojimbo talked. Alan Mendelsohn was looking a little pale, but I couldn't tell it if was the combination of the Regular chili and the second half of the cigar he had started before the meal, or if the fact of Clarence Yojimbo's otherworldliness had finally hit him.

"You see," Clarence Yojimbo was saying, "Rodni Rubenstein is perhaps one of the most annoying investigators of extraterrestrial phenomena—along with Erik VonDankninny, who's just as bad. These fellows have almost the right idea, but they go about it all wrong. Rodni Rubenstein has the awful habit of tinkering around with the material he gets ahold of in order to make his arguments more convincing. What he did to my dictionary is just a shame."

"You mean that what these boys told me is false?" Samuel Klugarsh asked. "Do you mean that you cannot, by reading *Yojimbo's Japanese-English Dictionary* backwards, noting only the second word in English in each entry, discover the ancient thought control methods of old Lemuria?"

"Of course you can," said Clarence Yojimbo. "And if you multiply the area of the base of the Great Pyramid of Cheops by your grandmother's height in centimeters, add two, and take away today's market price of chopped liver, you'll get either pi or the distance from the earth to the sun—I forget which. It doesn't prove a thing. You can't use Earth methods to solve unEarthly problems. It's like trying to fix an automobile engine by giving it an aspirin—although there are some rare cases where that will work—anyway, you see what I mean."

"I see what's happening," Dr. Prince said.

It's about time, I thought.

Dr. Prince was staring at the steamy window. He had a funny expression—sort of a bitter smile. "I've lost my mind. It's strange that I didn't notice it coming on. Here I am, smoking my pipe and listening to a fellow have a conversation with a Venusian motorcyclist, just as though it were the most natural thing in the world. Here I am, sitting in a place where I've just eaten something called Green Death chili, with one of my patients who has classic paranoid fantasies, and I'm just going along with the whole thing as if it were all true. It even makes sense to me. I'm a very sick man."

It was obvious that Dr. Prince wasn't talking to any of us. He was just staring at the window, out of which you couldn't see a thing, and babbling on.

"I assure you, you're imagining none of this," Clarence Yojimbo said.

"Why should I believe you?" Dr. Prince said. "You're a figment of the imagination. You're not even a figment of my imagination. You're a figment of Leonard's imagination. Why should I believe a figment?" Dr. Prince was starting to cry.

"I think our colleague is a little upset," Samuel Klugarsh said.

"I agree," said Clarence Yojimbo. "Perhaps we should bring this evening's discussion to an end. I'll see to it that Doctor Prince gets home all right, and I'll administer a Lemurian substance that will cause him to forget everything he's heard. We can meet again at your shop tomorrow. There are some things we really have to clear up."

The brothers of the Laughing Alligator escorted Dr. Prince, who kept saying "Crazy as a coot! Crazy as a coot!" out of the Bermuda Triangle Chili Parlor. They hoisted him onto a motorcycle and roared off into the darkness. Samuel Klugarsh arranged with Alan Mendelsohn and me to meet at his book shop the following day, right after school.

Alan Mendelsohn and I walked back to the bus station. We didn't say much. Seeing Dr. Prince go nuts was a little upsetting for both of us.

We were in luck—a bus for West Kangaroo Park was just about to leave. It was getting pretty late, and we were afraid that our parents might have telephoned each other and discovered we were missing. As it turned out, we got back just in time. Both mothers said that they were just about to telephone.

I had a hard time getting to sleep that night. I kept going over the things that had happened in the Bermuda Triangle Chili Parlor.

In the morning, I got a telephone call from Dr. Prince before I left for school. "Leonard, I just wanted to let you know that I won't be able to meet with you next week," he said.

"Is anything wrong?" I asked.

"No, no, nothing is wrong. I just want to take some time off. I'm going to visit my sister in Lemuria—I mean Bermuda—I mean San Diego. I've been working too hard and I need a rest."

"Have a nice trip, Doctor Prince," I said.

"Waka Waka," Dr. Prince said.

26

We were the first kids out of Bat Masterson Junior High School when the bell rang. The bus rolled up, and we got on.

We half-walked, half-trotted from the bus station to Samuel Klugarsh's shop. The Laughing Alligator motorcycles were parked outside. In the front part of the shop, the brothers of the Laughing Alligator were leafing through the books and giggling. They winked and nodded to us as we came in. In the back of the shop, Samuel Klugarsh and Clarence Yojimbo were sitting on folding chairs. They were drinking hot chocolate with double marshmallows and whipped cream from paper containers. Apparently they had sent out to the Bermuda Triangle Chili Parlor.

"Ah, there you are, boys," Samuel Klugarsh said. "Clarence Yojimbo has only been here a little while. Your hot chocolate is still hot, although, I'm afraid the marshmallows have completely melted by this time." He offered us two of the cardboard containers.

I noticed that the cover was off the Test Your Brainpower machine. Apparently, Samuel Klugarsh had been testing Clarence Yojimbo's brainpower before we arrived. The tube in which the red liquid rose to show you how advanced you were had melted, and the red stuff had dribbled all over the front of the machine.

The file cabinet drawers were open, and Samuel Klugarsh's mimeographed courses were all over the place. Also, the old-time radios and other scientific equipment looked as though they had been given a workout. Samuel Klugarsh's polka-dot bow tie was crooked, and he had spilled some hot chocolate on his pink shirt.

"We've been going over some of Mr. Klugarsh's research and educational material," Clarence Yojimbo said. "I was able to point out quite a few things that will have to be corrected immediately, isn't that right, Sam?"

"Absolutely, yes sir, this very day, sir," Samuel Klugarsh said. "Can I run out and get you some more hot chocolate? A cheeseburger? The contents of my savings account? Havana cigars?"

"Thank you," Clarence Yojimbo said, "I don't require anything at this time. Why don't you just take a chair and rest? I have to discuss a few things with Alan and Leonard."

"Yes, sir. Thank you. I'll sit down, now. Thank you," Samuel Klugarsh said. He seemed to be trying very hard to be extra polite to Clarence Yojimbo.

"Now, boys, let me bring you up to date. It seems that our friend, Mr. Klugarsh, has made somewhat the same error as that of Rodni Rubenstein, and other psychic and extraterrestrial scholars. He's become aware of certain things, but doesn't understand their use or significance. It's a little like this: Suppose there was no such thing as an automobile, and you came upon a good-as-new 1961 Studebaker Lark, all gassed up and ready to go. You'd call everybody to come and marvel at your discovery—but instead of realizing that it was a machine which had the power to carry people from place to place, suppose you and everyone else thought the purpose of that 1961 Studebaker Lark was to sit in the front seat and play the radio. You'd have pretty much missed the point, don't you agree?"

"Sure," we said.

"Thank you for referring to me as your friend," Samuel Klugarsh said.

"Well this is what has happened to students of strange phenomena," Clarence Yojimbo said. "Erik VonDankninny somehow guessed that persons from other planets have been visiting the earth for many thousands of years—but then he mixes us up with pyramids, and cave paintings, and, of all things, the history of religion. Utter nonsense. And Rodni Rubenstein seems to have found out that in some places, large rocks, and so forth, can be moved by mental power—and he makes the assumption that this is something that Earth people should be able to do as well. Then he goes ahead and doctors certain books, like my dictionary, to support his ideas. All very shocking."

"Shocking," Samuel Klugarsh said.

"And our friend, Mr. Klugarsh . . ."

"Thank you," said Samuel Klugarsh.

". . . packages the stuff and sells it to people—believing, of course, that he is doing nothing wrong."

"I swear," said Samuel Klugarsh.

"But, you see, it is very wrong. It would only be foolish to discover a brand-new 1961 Studebaker Lark and mistake it for a machine for listening to the radio—but to encourage people to do Mind Control stunts is much more than foolish. It is very dangerous."

"Dangerous," said Samuel Klugarsh. "Now you boys listen to Mr. Yojimbo."

"But we didn't do anything evil," Alan Mendelsohn said.

"That's right," I said, "we were just having fun. We wouldn't have used our powers to hurt anyone."

"Except yourselves," Clarence Yojimbo said. "If you got the idea that all these powers were good for was tricks, then you'd be limited forever from ever finding out what their real uses were. You'd end up like . . ." He looked at Samuel Klugarsh, "like Rodni Rubenstein."

"Mr. Yojimbo, is that chair comfortable?" Samuel Klugarsh asked. "I have a nice easy chair at home. I could get it."

"I'm fine just like this," Clarence Yojimbo said. "Now I want to explain everything to these boys. You see, you are the first people, regular Earth people, ever to attain what Mr. Klugarsh calls state twenty-six at will. Other people have attained it, but only at certain moments, and by accident. Somehow, from Klugarsh's moronic instructions, you've learned how to turn it on and off like a light switch. Now, while it's perfectly true that a person in state twenty-six can, to some extent, transmit his thoughts, and get people and even objects to do his bidding, that's not really what state twenty-six is good for. The point of state twenty-six is not to make yourself into a radio transmitter—but to make yourself into a radio receiver. In other words, instead of trying to put out messages, you should be picking them up. It's much more useful, and much more interesting."

"Well, we had sort of begun to get bored with giving people commands," Alan Mendelsohn said.

"That's when we got into levitating bricks and such," I put in.

"And you would have gotten bored with levitating bricks, and even whole houses soon," Clarence Yojimbo said. "Some people never get bored with stupid games—but usually when a person gets to be able to do something pointless, like transmit his thoughts, he soon realizes just how dull it is. Now tell me the truth: Except for some boorish mischief, can you think of any good use for sending mental commands?"

We couldn't.

"But what about moving objects by mental power?" I asked. "That could be useful for putting up buildings and things like that, couldn't it?"

"Why do you suppose God gave us hands, and brains that can figure out how to do things?" the Venusian said. "You know, there are people who believe that the pyramids and the Easter Island statues were erected by some kind of magic power that the ancient people learned from extraterrestrials. The reason they think this is because it hurts their pride that they can't figure out how it was done. They don't want to believe that some ancient Easter Islander knew as much about engineering as they do. But none of that stuff about spacemen building the great monuments of the ancient world is true. All those things were done by humans using their human gifts—including, but not depending on, moments of inspiration or intuition, or state twenty-six as Sam here calls it."

"Now, I want to explain about Mu, and Atlantis, and Lemuria, and Nafsulia, and Waka-Waka—all those lost continents. This is going to be a little tricky to understand, so feel free to ask questions as I go along. None of them were ever lost."

"You mean none of them ever existed?" I asked.

"All of them existed, and still do. They aren't exactly continents—but they exist. Oh, they're not called Waka-Waka or Atlantis—those are just made-up names for them—but they're real."

"Where are they?" Alan Mendelsohn asked.

"Here," Clarence Yojimbo said, "right here."

He was right. It was tricky to understand, and we said so.

"I'll explain. Maybe you've read about excavations of ancient cities—like Troy. After the archaeologists dig down and find the ancient city, sometimes they find that there's another still more ancient city underneath. Then they find that there's another city underneath that one—even more ancient. They find layers, levels. The so-called lost continents, or lost societies, are a little like that."

"Do you mean that if we dug straight down, we'd find Atlantis?" Alan Mendelsohn asked.

"If you dug straight down, you'd find the Hogboro Municipal Sewer," Clarence Yojimbo said. "To find Atlantis, you'd have to dig straight down within yourself."

"So Atlantis exists in our imagination—our memory?" I asked.

"If you like," Clarence Yojimbo said. "I prefer to believe that it exists outside us, but we can only find it by going inside."

"I'm getting confused," Alan Mendelsohn said.

"So am I," I said.

"I've been confused since last night," Samuel Klugarsh said. "How about we break for a snack? I can run around the corner for some frozen yogurt for us and the Laughing Alligator brothers—by the way, how are they doing out there?"

We peeked into the front of the store. The brothers of the Laughing Alligator were taking turns reading a Scientology book to each other and cracking up laughing.

"Reynold and Hamilton will go with you to help bring back the yogurt," Clarence Yojimbo said. "It's a good idea—I'm getting dry from all this talking."

27

While Samuel Klugarsh was gone, Clarence Yojimbo went around the room tapping all the scientific gadgets. He seemed to be listening to the taps—he'd keep tapping until he was satisfied, and then move on to another machine. I couldn't hear any difference between the taps.

"Most of your instruments were out of adjustment," he said to Samuel Klugarsh when he returned. "I've got them pretty well tuned up for you. Just try not to move them around too much—they're pretty primitive and delicate.

"Now," Clarence Yojimbo continued, between bites of yogurt, "I'm going to explain to all of you about the so-called lost continents. It seems we weren't making much progress before, so I'm going to try to just blast right along, and maybe you'll get a general idea. People tend to believe only what they can see—that's perfectly natural and reasonable. But what if everybody saw in black and white and you could see colors? Chances are, no one would believe that colors existed. They might think you were crazy if you kept talking about colors. But the colors would exist just the same, even if not everybody could see them. Everybody with me so far?"

We were.

"Suppose I told you that I could see something that you couldn't see? Taking into account that I'm a Venusian, and have already demonstrated that I am able to know things which I have no way of knowing—like the fact that today Samuel Klugarsh's undershorts are white with little red hearts on them . . ."

"That's absolutely right!" Samuel Klugarsh said.

". . . would you be willing to concede, just for the sake of argument, that I can see things which ordinary Earth people can't see?"

"Yes."

"OK."

"That's reasonable."

"OK," Clarence Yojimbo continued. "Having granted that I am able to see things that you can't, and having noticed that I am really a nice guy, besides which, I have no reason to lie to you, are you willing to believe that, in addition to us four, there are others in this room?"

For some reason this idea struck me as sort of scary. I felt a shiver.

"In fact," Clarence Yojimbo said, "there are a whole lot of people in this room. There are some people about nine feet tall, sitting around and drinking cups of fleegix. There are also some people walking through here on their way to someplace else. There are also some people cooking. There are also some people making tables and chairs out of wood. There are also some people sleeping.

"What's more, the people drinking fleegix can't see us or the people walking, the people cooking, the people working, or the people sleeping. The people walking can't see us or the people drinking fleegix, or the people cooking, or the people working, or the people sleeping. Are you starting to get the picture?"

"What's fleegix?" Alan Mendelsohn asked.

"It's a hot drink, similar to hot chocolate, usually served in a cup with two marshmallows and whipped cream," Clarence Yojimbo said. "But that's not the point. The point is that in the same space, there are at least six different bunches of people—or beings—doing different things, and not interfering with any of the other bunches of people—or beings."

"What has this got to do with lost continents?" Samuel Klugarsh wanted to know.

"Wait a minute!" Alan Mendelsohn said. "I think I've got it! Those places where the others are—drinking fleegix, walking, working, and so forth—those *are* the lost continents!"

"You've got it," Clarence Yojimbo said.

"But continents are places," Samuel Klugarsh said. "I've got at least fifteen books in the front of the shop that tell how there's proof that these continents used to exist. How did all those people get into that ghostlike state? Did they die, or what?"

"One of the reasons," Clarence Yojimbo said, "that you haven't got a bigger, more successful, mystical, occult book shop, is that you read all the books. What makes you think that the people I'm telling you about are in a ghostlike state, in limbo? What do you suppose they'd say if I appeared before them and told them that the three of you are sitting here, in the back of a book shop?"

"They'd think we were like ghosts?" Samuel Klugarsh said.

"Of course they would," Clarence Yojimbo said. "They can't see you; they can't hear you; they can't feel, smell, or taste you. If I could persuade them to take my word for your being here at all, the best they could do would be to assume that you were insubstantial, like spirits—but you're not, are you?"

Samuel Klugarsh scratched his head, "No, I'm really here."

"And they're really there," Clarence Yojimbo said. "If you go to some tribe in the Amazon River jungle and tell them all about Los Angeles, California, they're going to have a hard time believing you. Even if you show them pictures, the best they're going to be able to do is fix up their idea of Los Angeles, California, so that it fits in with their everyday experience."

"Mr. Yojimbo," Alan Mendelsohn said, "how come

you can see all this stuff? Is it because you are a Venusian?"

"That's right," Clarence Yojimbo said. "Obviously, people from other planets are going to have extra powers that Earth people don't have. Anybody who has ever watched television knows that. But—and this is interesting—there has always been contact between these different, let's call them planes of existence. That's where all the stories about Atlantis and Mu and Lemuria and Nafsulia and Waka-Waka came from in the first place. People from this plane of existence have stumbled on information from one or more of the other ones. Sometimes they even get a quick look."

"How does that happen?" I asked.

"Well, it's like this," Clarence Yojimbo said. "Right now, I'm sort of tuned in on Nafsulia; that's the plane I described on which people are walking from one place to another. It so happens that this room is right in the middle of the main street of Nafsu City. It's four o'clock in the afternoon on a business day—the Nafsulians have the same sort of time sequences as you do—so hundreds and thousands of people have passed through this room all day long. Not one of them has noticed that he or she is walking through a room. Maybe one in five thousand will have a funny sensation, just for a second, while walking through here. Maybe one in ten thousand will have a funny sensation and pay any attention to it. Maybe one in a hundred thousand will suspect they have come into contact with something not visible in their ordinary world—but they won't quite know what it is. One in a million, or fewer, will actually have a pretty good idea of what's going on when they walk through this room—and maybe one in ten million, at the most, will actually get a glimpse of us. And that one in ten million won't be able to glimpse us every time he comes this way. It will just happen at random, maybe a few times in his life. Now, one Nafsulian in a hundred million will be able to really see what's going on here, just as clearly as I can see all of them. If that Nafsulian tells the other

Nafsulians what he's seen, they'll take him to the booby
hatch. He's a pretty intelligent fellow, so he doesn't say
anything.

"Now that intelligent Nafsulian gets a look, one day,
at—let's say, the Bermuda Triangle Chili Parlor. Chili is
unknown in Nafsulia, although they have all the ingredi-
ents to make it. He watches the owner of the Bermuda
Triangle Chili Parlor make up a batch of Green Death
chili. He sees how it's done, and he makes some too. The
other Nafsulians love it. But they also know that nothing
of the kind has ever existed or been thought of in Nafsulia.
They want to know how the fellow who made it got the
idea. He tells them they made chili like that in Hogboro.
Where's Hogboro? It isn't on any Nafsulian map. Nobody ever heard of it. Yet there's the chili. It had to
come from somewhere. Are you getting the picture?"

"Yes," I said. "The Nafsulians assume that if Hogboro
doesn't exist now, it must have existed in the past. Since
it doesn't exist anymore, something must have happened
to it."

"So they make up a story," Alan Mendelsohn broke in,
"about how Hogboro used to be a mighty continent, but
it sank into the ocean."

"That's it exactly!" Clarence Yojimbo said. "Now, why
am I bothering to tell you all this?"

"Because you like us?" Samuel Klugarsh said.

"Because I like you, and something more important,"
Clarence Yojimbo said. "A while ago, I told Alan and
Leonard that they were the first Earth people ever to be
able to turn what you call state twenty-six on and off at
will. I also told them that using that power to do simple
tricks was wrong because it would cause them to be
unable to find out what that power was really good for.

"What that power is good for is to enable a person to
see and hear what is happening on the other planes of
existence. That's how Venusians do it. Any person equipped
with what you call state twenty-six can learn to travel in
and out of the various parallel planes of existence. Re-

member, I said that some people have always been able to experience state twenty-six at random moments. Those are the people who get little blips from the other planes of existence. Even the guy who discovered Green Death chili couldn't do such a thing at will. But these two boys can learn to do it just the way I do."

"By the way, Mr. Yojimbo," Alan Mendelsohn asked, "how exactly did you get to Earth?"

"A good question," Clarence Yojimbo said. "I come from the sixth existential plane on Venus. To get from the sixth existential plane on Venus to the Waka-Waka plane on Earth is as easy as taking a bus to West Kangaroo Park where you guys live. Then equipped with what you call state twenty-six, I can come from the Waka-Waka plane directly to this one. If I want to, I can get back to my home plane on Venus in about an hour and twenty minutes—which I don't want to do, because they're having a terrific snowstorm there right now."

"Do you mean to say we can do that too?" I asked.

"When you learn how," Clarence Yojimbo said.

"How do we learn how?"

"Read my book."

28

"Your book? Do you mean *Yojimbo's Japanese-English Dictionary?*" Alan Mendelsohn asked.

"That's the only book I ever wrote," Clarence Yojimbo said. "It explains, step by step, how to observe and even visit other planes of existence."

"But you said that following the instructions in the book was wrong," I said.

"It's wrong if you read the book backwards, noting only the second word in English in each entry," Clarence Yojimbo said. "That was the idea of that so-called scholar, Rodni Rubenstein. The right way to read the book is front to back, using The Key—then you get the instructions in Interplanar Existential Communication."

"Good Lord, how I admire this man!" Samuel Klugarsh said.

"The Key?" Alan Mendelsohn and I asked.

"The Key that comes with the book. Didn't you sell them a copy of The Key with the book?" Clarence Yojimbo asked Samuel Klugarsh.

"I never heard of The Key," Samuel Klugarsh said. "All I ever saw was the dictionary. That's all Mr. Rubenstein sold me along with the course in Hyperstellar Archaeology."

"Well, you've got to have a Key—otherwise, the book is no good," Clarence Yojimbo said.

"Where can we get a Key?" Alan Mendelsohn asked.

"It so happens, I've got one with me," Clarence Yojimbo said. "I'd really like to give it to you, but they're very expensive to produce. The Laughing Alligator brothers and I have expenses to meet, you see—I mean, even a Venusian needs money to get around. There's gas for the motorcycles, and food, and all sorts of things."

"Could you sell us The Key?" Alan Mendelsohn asked.

"Well, yes," Clarence Yojimbo said. "That hadn't occurred to me—I mean, I'm really interested in your developing your powers to their highest potential—but that would be the best way."

"How much would you want for The Key?" I asked. There was something strangely familiar about all this.

"Let's see," Clarence Yojimbo said. "The last time I sold a copy of The Key, it was to Rodni Rubenstein. I charged him, now let me see . . ." Clarence Yojimbo took a little notebook out of his jacket pocket and thumbed through it. "Ah! Here it is. I sold him the dictionary and The Key for six thousand dollars."

"We could never pay six thousand dollars," I said.

"Of course not," Clarence Yojimbo said, "and this is entirely different. All I want from you boys is enough for the Laughing Alligators and me to get to New York City— you probably didn't know that we've got a folk-singing group. We sing Venusian and Waka-Wakian folk songs, and we've got an offer to do a week at a folk club in New York. All we'll need, is, let me see . . ." He dug a pencil out of his pocket and did some figuring in his notebook. "One hundred forty-two dollars and fifty cents—how's that sound?"

"Like six thousand," I said.

"Really, I couldn't do it for a penny less," Clarence Yojimbo said. "What's more, we have to start out tomorrow if we're going to get to New York in time. I was planning to maybe go back to the sixth existential plane of Venus tonight, and see if I could borrow the money from my brother—but I really don't want to, with the snowstorm and all. Besides, my brother is mad at me because I haven't paid him back the money I borrowed for the motorcycles."

"I just don't know where we'd get a hundred and forty-two fifty," I said.

"My comic collection is worth a lot more than that," Alan Mendelsohn said, "but I don't know where I could sell it fast."

"William Lloyd Floyd at Morrie's bookstore buys comics," Samuel Klugarsh said. "Maybe he would be willing to make a fast deal."

"I'll tell you what," Clarence Yojimbo said, "I'll take a chance. I won't go to the sixth existential plane of Venus tonight. Instead, I'll wait until tomorrow, and meet you here at two o'clock sharp. Then, if you've been able to raise the money, we'll leave for New York straight from here. If you can't do it, I'll go to see my brother, and we'll just have to break the speed laws getting to New York the following day. Fair enough?"

We said we guessed so.

"OK, we'll meet tomorrow," Clarence Yojimbo said. "Now I've got to go and rehearse with the Laughing Alligators." He headed for the door. "Waka Waka!" he said.

"Waka Waka," we all replied.

29

Something I had never done before was cut school. It was easier than I had ever suspected. At lunchtime, we just walked out. I figured none of my teachers would report me absent, since they never noticed me anyway. In Alan's case, they would be so grateful he wasn't there, they weren't likely to look into the matter. In any event, even if we got into trouble later, this was important.

The tricky part was sneaking into Alan Mendelsohn's basement, where he had his treasured comic collection stuffed into two big cartons, waiting by the door. His mother was home, so we had to sneak by her. Luckily, she was vacuuming, and the noise covered any sounds we might have made. The cartons were large and very heavy. I could hardly walk with mine. Each of them contained over a thousand comics. By the time we hoisted them onto the Hogboro bus and flopped into our seats, we were sweating and out of breath.

I felt sort of bad that Alan Mendelsohn was putting up all the money for The Key to *Yojimbo's Japanese-English Dictionary*. He said that this was no time to quibble over details—besides, he thought that after we had gotten good at traveling to other existential planes, we could sell the whole works to Samuel Klugarsh. And he made me promise to go around with him and help him rebuild his collection when we had some time. I told him I would be happy to do that.

When the bus pulled into Hogboro, we dragged our

cartons off and started out for Morrie's Bookstore. It was hard work. The cartons were too big to get a good hold of, and Alan Mendelsohn kept telling me not to let my carton drop—he didn't want any of the comics to get crumpled. We had to stop and rest twice in every block.

We finally got to Morrie's Bookstore. We opened the door and pushed the cartons of comics across the floor to William Lloyd Floyd's desk.

"What are those, comics?" he asked.

"Yeah," Alan Mendelsohn panted. "We heard that you buy collections."

"I love comics!" William Lloyd Floyd said. "Let me see them!"

He dove at the cartons hungrily. He pulled out handfuls of comic books, and whistled, and hummed, and talked to himself. "Wow! *Fantastic Eleven* Number 6—I've always wanted that one! Hey, you've got a complete run of *The Avenging Chicken*, including Number 1. This is a great collection! Oh look! *Bloody War Stories!* That's really great!"

I never really understood why some people get so excited about comics. I mean, they're all right when there's nothing else, but William Lloyd Floyd was really going out of his mind over Alan Mendelsohn's collection.

"Oooo! Ooo! *Superduck!* I love *Superduck!* These for sale? Tell you what—I'll give you ten dollars for each box, OK?"

Alan Mendelsohn didn't say anything.

"Oh! Oh! *The Avenging Chipmunk!* I've never seen *The Avenging Chipmunk;* it's really rare. Oh! I've got to have this."

William Lloyd Floyd was sitting on the floor pulling handfuls of comics out of the two cartons. Alan Mendelsohn looked completely cool. I was sweating. I was wondering how Alan Mendelsohn would get the price from ten dollars for each carton to one hundred forty-two fifty.

"Oh! *Dr. Unpleasant!*" William Lloyd Floyd shouted.

"You've got every issue of *Dr. Unpleasant!* Oh, I really have to have this!"

At the picnic table in the back of the store, the Mad Guru was playing three simultaneous games of chess against himself. Alan Mendelsohn was totally relaxed. William Lloyd Floyd was nearly crazy.

"Would you sell me just the series of *Dr. Unpleasant?*" he asked.

"The whole thing," Alan Mendelsohn said.

"OK, the whole thing," William Lloyd Floyd said. "Oh look! *The Mad Goon! Nobody* has *The Mad Goon!* If I give you two and a half cents per book, there's about two thousand here—how about fifty bucks?"

"No," Alan Mendelsohn said.

"OK, a hundred," William Lloyd Floyd said.

"Did you notice that I've got *Roosman the Barbarian,* Numbers 1 through 12?" Alan Mendelsohn asked.

"One hundred and ten dollars, and that's my final offer!" William Lloyd Floyd said.

"Let's go, Leonard," Alan Mendelsohn said, and he began gathering up the comics.

"Wait!" William Lloyd Floyd shouted. "I'll give you my top price, nine and one-quarter cents a book—that comes to a hundred and eighty-five dollars. I haven't got a cent more than that to my name."

"Throw in the potato?" Alan Mendelsohn asked.

"What? My brass potato from the moon? It's worth millions!"

"I've also got here, *Wonder Wombat* from the nineteen thirties, in perfect condition," Alan Mendelsohn said.

"*Wonder Wombat?*" William Lloyd Floyd shouted. "Show me."

Alan Mendelsohn dug out a copy of an old comic in a plastic envelope. "It's the first issue," he said, showing it to William Lloyd Floyd.

"Take the potato!" William Lloyd Floyd said, and he

slipped the leather thong off his neck. He rummaged around in his desk drawer and pants pockets, and borrowed six dollars from the Mad Guru, finally coming up with one hundred and eighty-five dollars.

Alan Mendelsohn and I walked out of the store with enough to pay for The Key to Interplanar Existential Communication, with forty-two fifty left over and a brass potato from the moon.

"The difference between that man and me," Alan Mendelsohn said, "is that I am a connoisseur, and he is a fanatic."

30

"Hey! Alan and Leonard!" Clarence Yojimbo seemed glad to see us. "We were worried you wouldn't . . . I mean . . . I'm glad to see that you . . . uh, did you get the money?"

"Sure," Alan Mendelsohn said.

"See?" Clarence Yojimbo shouted to the Laughing Alligators, who were milling around inside Samuel Klugarsh's bookstore. "What did I tell you?"

We noticed a bunch of bags, suitcases, and things that looked like they might contain guitars and banjos, piled just inside the door of the bookstore.

"The Laughing Alligator brothers were worried that we might not be able to go to New York," Clarence Yojimbo said. "See, you guys? It's all right. I told you so," he shouted to the bikers.

"Mr. Yojimbo, about The Key," Alan Mendelsohn said.

"Oh, yes—The Key—I've got it right here." Clarence Yojimbo pulled a thick manila envelope out of his leather jacket. "That will be one hundred forty-two dollars and fifty cents," he said. "We'll forget about the Venusian sales tax."

Clarence Yojimbo handed Alan Mendelsohn the envelope, and Alan Mendelsohn handed him one hundred forty-two dollars and fifty cents.

"Well, that's that," the Venusian said. "Look, I hate long good-byes. Me and the Laughing Alligators will just split, OK?" He started for the door.

"Wait!" I shouted. "How do we use this Key?"

141

"All the instructions are in the envelope," Clarence Yojimbo said. "Bye." He went through the door, followed by the brothers of the Laughing Alligator.

All this time, Samuel Klugarsh hadn't said anything. He had just stood around in various corners. Now he stepped forward. "Do you boys mind if I have a look at The Key?" he said.

The front door opened, and Clarence Yojimbo stuck his head in. "And don't show that thing to Samuel Klugarsh," he said. "Don't even open it here. Just get it home where it will be safe. Bye again!" and he was gone.

"Just a peek," Samuel Klugarsh said.

"We've got to be going now, Mr. Klugarsh," I said.

"Just let me feel it," Samuel Klugarsh said.

"Let's get out of here," Alan Mendelsohn said.

When we got out into the street, we could still hear the roar of the motorcycles of the Laughing Alligators and Clarence Yojimbo, the Venusian, and we could still see the blue smoke from their engines as they headed for the interstate highway.

We headed straight for the bus station. Neither of us spoke until we were locked in Alan Mendelsohn's bedroom.

Alan Mendelsohn put the manila envelope on his desk and flopped on his bed. I sat down in Alan's desk chair, having pulled it back so both of us could look at the envelope. Neither of us talked for a long time.

"Well, we've got The Key," I said, finally.

"Yes, it's right there in that envelope," Alan Mendelsohn said.

"Communicating with other planes of existence should be very exciting," I said.

"Yes," Alan Mendelsohn said.

"It sure cost a lot of money," I said.

"Sure did," Alan Mendelsohn said.

"Do you think it's going to work?" I asked.

"There's only one way to find out," Alan Mendelsohn said.

"Right," I said. "Go ahead. Open it."

"No. You," Alan Mendelsohn said.

"You paid for it," I said.

"You open it," Alan Mendelsohn said.

There was something heavy and stiff inside the envelope. I carefully undid the little metal clasp and peeled back the glued flap. Then I slid out a whole bunch of sheets of smooth, thin brown cardboard with lots of little rectangular slits cut in them. There was a typewritten sheet too:

INSTRUCTIONS

In this envelope you will find a whole bunch of sheets of smooth, thin brown cardboard with lots of little rectangular slits in them. This is The Key to *Yojimbo's Japanese-English Dictionary*. You will notice that each sheet has two numbers on it—one red and one black. The black number tells you in what order to use the sheet—1, 2, 3, 4, 5, 6, and so forth. The red number tells you which page in the dictionary the sheet corresponds to—for example, page 146 (the red number) corresponds to sheet 1 (the black number).

The sheets are exactly the same size as the pages of the dictionary. Place the appropriate sheet carefully over the page, with the numbers facing you, and certain words and phrases will appear in the slits. Copy these down in a notebook—this will create your copy of The Key. Be sure to hide the sheets and the dictionary in separate places, so no one can decipher the secret message in the dictionary, even if they find one or the other. Also, guard the notebook with the deciphered Key with your life. Best of luck. Burn this.

"Well, let's get started," Alan Mendelsohn said. He got a fresh notebook. "You read, and I'll write," he said.

I put sheet number 1 (the black number) carefully over page 146 (the red number) and read off the words visible through the slits to Alan Mendelsohn, who copied them down in the notebook. We went fairly fast, not really paying too much attention to what we were reading and copying. When we were all done, Alan Mendelsohn turned to the beginning of his notebook and read aloud.

31

THE KEY TO INTERPLANAR EXISTENTIAL COMMUNICATION

For centuries people have believed that once there existed continents, places, and whole civilizations, now lost through natural catastrophe or intervention from inhabitants of other planets. This is not so.

In fact there are a number of parallel planes of existence, which are happening right now under, over, and around us—but we can't see them. Only in moments of especially high intuition, or inspiration, can we be aware of these planes of existence— which, for purposes of reference, we will call by the names of the traditional lost continents: Atlantis, Mu, Lemuria, Nafsulia, Waka-Waka, and so forth.

The special mental attitude, or state of intuition, is sometimes called state twenty-six by modern psychic researchers—so we will use that term as well.

Ordinary people cannot experience state twenty-six just by wishing to do so. It is something that just happens at random—and sometimes, when it happens, we get a glimpse of one of the "lost continents" of extraplanar existence.

What this key, or guide, cannot do is tell anyone how to achieve state twenty-six. All that can be done is to point out the fact that there are certain physical places on this Earth where it appears to be easier to make contact (state twenty-six being present) with the other planes. There follows a list of such places. The experimenter is advised to go to one or all of them—and wait for state twenty-six to happen. Good Luck—Clarence Yojimbo, Venusian and folk singer.

32

"That's it? That's it? That's all it says for my one hundred and forty-two dollars? We've been swindled again!" Alan Mendelsohn was really worked up.

"Look," I said, "It might not be so bad. After all, Clarence Yojimbo said that we're the first people ever to be able to go in and out of state twenty-six at will. The least we should do is try it out."

"Well, I don't see that we've got much choice," Alan Mendelsohn said. "I mean, he's got my money, and he's on his way to New York with his motorcycling folk singers—but, boy this has me mad—this isn't even as interesting as those courses Klugarsh sold us."

"Which taught us to get into state twenty-six," I reminded Alan Mendelsohn, "and to transmit our thoughts."

"You may be right," Alan Mendelsohn said. "Let's have a look at the list."

The list was on a single page of the notebook. It said:

PLACES SUITABLE FOR INTERPLANAR CONTACT

Giant rock, Muhu, Estonia
Rampa's Kosher Deli, Heiho, Tibet
Mukerjee's Shoe Shop, Nainpur, India
Paleolithic formation, Tjidjulang, Java
Dead Flamingo Lake, Loitokitok, Kenya
Public library, Popovo, Bulgaria
42 Wishnik Street, Krasnik, Poland

Central sewer, Gruben, Switzerland
MacTavish's Fast Food and Opticians,
    Findhorn, Scotland
Akanakuji Temple, Ichikawa, Japan
Hergeschleimer's Oriental Gardens,
    Hogboro, United States
Meteor crater, Fort Simpson,
    Northwest Territories

"We appear to be in luck," Alan Mendelsohn said.
"The only location in the United States is right here in
Hogboro."

"That's right," I said. "The next closest spot is the
meteor crater in Fort Simpson, Northwest Territories,
Canada."

"Where is this Hergeschleimer's Oriental Gardens?"
Alan Mendelsohn wanted to know.

"Search me. I've never heard of it," I said. "How
about checking the telephone book?"

We looked for Hergeschleimer's Oriental Gardens in
the Hogboro telephone directory. There was nothing
under *Hergeschleimer*, *Gardens*, or *Oriental* in the yellow or white pages.

"It could be Hergeschleimer's Oriental Gardens doesn't
have a phone," I said.

Alan Mendelsohn remembered a book he'd bought in
a bookstore in The Bronx when he heard his family was
moving to Hogboro. He dug out a cardboard carton from
the back of his closet, and rummaged around in it. He
came up with a tattered old paperback. "This is a tourist
guide to Hogboro," he said, "published in 1932. Let's
see if it mentions Hergeschleimer's Oriental Gardens."
We looked in the index and table of contents. We looked
at the map of Hogboro with little pictures of monuments
and places of interest. There was nothing about Hergeschleimer's Oriental Gardens.

Alan Mendelsohn tossed the book onto my lap. "I'm

really disgusted," he said. "There's no such place as Hergeschleimer's Oriental Gardens."

I looked at the book. The cover was printed in yellow and black. *Tourist Guide to Hogboro*, it said. The rest of the cover was taken up with a picture of a bunch of postcards. The postcards were all together in a pile, and you could only really make out four or five of them—the rest were covered by other postcards. At the bottom of each postcard, in the narrow white margin, was printed whatever the postcard showed, the War Memorial, City Hall, Fleegle Street at Night, and one of the partially covered postcards bore the lettering ——hleimer's Oriental Gardens.

"Hey, look at this!" I shouted.

Alan Mendelsohn looked at the cover. He scrunched up his face and peered at it from one inch away. There wasn't much doubt that ——hleimer's Oriental Gardens would say Hergeschleimer's Oriental Gardens, if the postcard covering it were moved away.

"So it does exist!" Alan Mendelsohn shouted. "But why doesn't the book mention it? It's on the cover."

We went through the book again, page by page. Nowhere was there any mention of Hergeschleimer's Oriental Gardens.

"Look at this," Alan Mendelsohn said, pointing to the copyright page. "This book was first printed in 1932, and reprinted in 1951. If you look closely at the pictures of postcards on the cover, you'll notice that all the cars are old-time nineteen twenties types."

"So you think that Hergeschleimer's Oriental Gardens may have ceased to exist sometime between 1932 and 1951?" I asked.

"It looks that way," Alan Mendelsohn said, "but the *place* is still there. My guess is that it's the place that makes the interplanar communication possible—not what's in the place. We have to find out where Hergeschleimer's Oriental Gardens *were!*"

He was starting to cheer up and get interested again, now that we had some detective work to do.

The following day ws spent trying to find out where Hergeschleimer's Oriental Gardens (whatever they were) had been. None of our teachers knew anything about them. My parents didn't remember ever having heard of them. The school library was no help, and neither was the branch of the public library. We called the *Hogboro Tribune*—they didn't know either. We were stuck. Then my father had a good suggestion. "Why don't you ask Uncle Boris?"

Uncle Boris had been a taxi driver once, and he was a sort of amateur Hogboro historian. He was more likely to know about Hergeschleimer's Oriental Gardens than anybody.

I phoned Alan Mendelsohn, and told him that I was going to arrange for us to eat supper at my grandparents' house the next night. There was no point to telephoning Uncle Boris to ask about Hergeschleimer's Oriental Gardens, because he had a terror of telephones. You had to see him in person.

33

Eating supper at my grandparents' house is a unique experience. First of all, the Old One believes that people shouldn't eat regular meals three times a day. She thinks that's unhealthy. She thinks you should eat something whenever you're hungry. This means that the people who live in the apartment just wander into the kitchen whenever they want, and take some food, and eat it there, or eat it while walking around, or settle down someplace and eat. The Old One is almost constantly in the kitchen, which is surprising when you consider that she believes everything ought to be eaten raw—so there's no actual cooking. I don't think she even has a stove—I know I've never seen one in use in her kitchen. But she has blenders, juicers, mixers, a grain mill, and two refrigerators. When she has all the electric equipment going at once, and the two refrigerators humming, it sounds like a shipyard, and the lights flicker throughout the rest of the apartment house.

She had a really interesting soup the night Alan Mendelsohn and I came for supper. It had ground-up cherries, and celery, and raw buckwheat groats in it, and a lot of other stuff I couldn't figure out. She also gave us something called tsampa that Madame Zelatnowa had made. It was OK. As usual there was a salad with everything in the world in it, and big gobs of homemade yogurt on top. She also served bean sprouts with sesame seeds and garlic and vinegar. Alan Mendelsohn liked that best. I'm not saying that I'd like to eat at the Old

One's house every day—but it isn't bad—and I do feel sort of good for hours after I've eaten every time I go there. Alan Mendelsohn had three helpings of everything.

Just as we were having our dessert of unbaked sesame, honey, coconut, carob, vegetable-protein cookies and cranberry juice, Uncle Boris walked in. He helped himself to a big bowl of raw oats with cashew nuts and carrot syrup and sat down at the kitchen table with us. "Hello boys," he said. "How's the psychic investigation?"

"That's what we came to talk to you about," I said. "You see, we met this Venusian . . ."

"No kidding!" Uncle Boris said. "A Venusian! That's really interesting. I met a Saturnian once, but we never got to be friends. He kept trying to eat my wristwatch. Was this Venusian friendly?"

"He was very friendly," I said. "He sold us a Key to *Yojimbo's Japanese-English Dictionary* that decodes instructions for getting in touch with parallel planes of existence—like invisible worlds. In order to make contact, we have to find a place called Hergeschleimer's Oriental Gardens, but it seems to have vanished. We can't find anyone who knows where it is, or was. We were hoping you'd be able to help us."

"Sure, I remember Hergeschleimer's Oriental Gardens," Uncle Boris said.

Alan Mendelsohn and I couldn't help jumping up and down in our chairs, like little kids.

"I used to go there a lot, years ago," my uncle continued. "It was really nice. You see, Lance Hergeschleimer was a fine man. He was a traveler and a botanist and a collector of wonderful things. His garden was a combination park, museum of rare tropical and Asiatic plants, and a nice place to have tea. He must have been very rich, because the place went on and on, and he had planted big trees, full-grown ones, from all sorts of distant places. Just getting them here alive and well must have cost a fortune. There were statues made of bronze and stone too—Buddhas and scenes of Asian village life.

He had Japanese sand gardens and little teahouses and pagodas. Oh, it was a wonderful place to go for a walk, years ago. You know, I made a movie of that place. Would you like to see it?"

We said we would like to see it very much, but did Uncle Boris happen to remember where Hergeschleimer's Oriental Gardens had been?

"You know, I've been trying to remember that," he said. "It wasn't right in town—but somewhere out in the country—you had to take a long, long streetcar ride to get there. Maybe it will come back to me when we're watching the film."

We followed Uncle Boris to his bedroom, which looked more like a storeroom. There were stacks and piles and mounds of all sorts of things—books, geological specimens, camera equipment, stuffed birds, hiking equipment, bundles of letters, clothing, paintings, tools, everything. Uncle Boris began dragging large cardboard cartons out of his closet. They were full of reels of movie film. On the side of each carton, Uncle Boris had written in black crayon the titles of the films in the box. He dragged out five or six cartons, and finally found the one with a film called *Hergeschleimer's Oriental Gardens, 1939*.

Uncle Boris was pretty old. He wasn't my regular uncle—like my father's brother or my mother's brother. I think he was the Old One's brother—or maybe he was the Old One's uncle. She called him Uncle Boris. He talked with an accent.

"Now," he said, "let's get the projector set up in the dining room, and we'll have a look at this film."

The very first shot in the film was a picture of a street sign. You could read the names of both cross streets, Nussbaum Street and Utopia Avenue.

"Those are out near my house!" I shouted.

"Well, I told you Hergeschleimer's Oriental Gardens were out in the country," Uncle Boris said. "When this film was taken, West Kangaroo Park did not exist. It was all woods and dairy farms and Hergeschleimer's Oriental Gardens—now watch the film."

The camera panned from the street sign to a big neon sign on a tall post. The sign wasn't turned on—it was daytime, but there were painted letters behind the neon tubes, HERGESCHLEIMER'S ORIENTAL GARDENS. There was no doubt—we know knew where the Oriental Gardens were located.

Then we saw pictures of beautiful trees and flowering plants. There were neat gravel paths leading among the wonderful trees and bushes. Then we saw Uncle Boris, looking a lot younger, dressed in a light brown suit with a straw hat, one of those flat ones, and spats! He had to explain to us about spats—they're like leggings, only they cover just part of your shoe. That didn't make any sense to us. Uncle Boris said they were snappy. He also had a tie with a palm tree on it. He said it was hand painted. Uncle Boris, in his suit and straw hat and spats and hand-painted tie, walked straight toward the camera, which didn't move. The last thing you saw was his nose. Then the movie showed more of the beautiful plants, and a pond. Then you saw Uncle Boris again, this time in a light blue suit, with different spats and a different hand-painted tie—same straw hat—walking into the camera again. Then you saw the gardens. Then you saw a black-and-white photograph in a little golden frame hanging in the leaves of some strange plant. You couldn't see what the picture was of because of the reflections in the glass—it looked like a person, or people. Then you saw Uncle Boris, in still another suit, spats, and hand-painted tie, walking into the camera. Then foliage. Then another black-and-white photograph hanging among the leaves. You still couldn't see what the picture showed, but you could see it was different from the first. Then Uncle Boris. Then foliage. Then a statue of a Buddha. Then foliage. Then black-and-white photos in little golden frames. Then foliage. It went on and on. It was strangely interesting.

Well, it wasn't interesting—but it was nice to look at. It was restful. Uncle Boris wouldn't explain why the different suits or what was in the black-and-white photos. "It's a work of art," he said. "You don't have to know what it means."

34

It was Saturday morning—the next day. Alan Mendelsohn and I started off on foot for Nussbaum Street and Utopia Avenue, right after breakfast. It was a long walk—it took almost an hour to get there.

Utopia Avenue is one of those big streets—a highway almost. Cars travel fairly fast, and the sides of the road are lined with chain stores and discount houses—Shoe Monster, MacTavish's Pickle-Burgers, Do-it-Yourself Swimming Pools, Intergalactic House of Waffles, and lots of gas stations. No sidewalks, of course—we walked along in the gutter with cars zooming past us.

At the intersection, we found a deserted diner, an auto muffler place, a gas station, and a little junkyard. None of it looked anything like Uncle Boris's movie. In the film, the whole area had been green and countrylike. Now it was all built up and dirty and noisy and smelling of automobile exhaust.

There was a tangle of old trees and bushes behind the junkyard—most of them looked dead.

"Do you suppose that could have been Hergeschleimer's Oriental Gardens?" I asked Alan Mendelsohn.

"It looks like our best bet," he said. "Let's go over and find out."

We crossed the road—that was hairy, with all the cars whizzing by. As we entered the junkyard gate, a very old German shepherd walked stiffly over to us and barked. It was more like a cough. We could see that he had very few teeth.

"Pretend you're afraid of him!" someone shouted. We saw that it was a little fat guy who had just come out of a little shack. "Please, otherwise his feelings will be hurt."

"Pretend we're afraid?" I asked.

"C'mon, do it," said the little fat guy. "It'll make him feel good."

I felt a little silly. "Oh, please don't bite me!" I said to the dog, who was yawning.

"Hey mister, call off this vicious dog!" Alan Mendelsohn said.

"That's enough, Fafner," the little fat guy called out. "Let them come in."

The dog staggered back to the car seat he'd been sleeping on, and crashed down onto it.

"Thanks for cooperating," the little fat guy said. "Fafner is pretty old, but I don't want him to feel useless. My name is Noel Wallaby. What can I do for you?"

"We wanted to know if this place was ever Herge-schleimer's Oriental Gardens," I said.

"My goodness," Noel Wallaby said, "I didn't think anybody remembered Hergeschleimer's Oriental Gardens—especially not anybody your age. Yes, this was where the teahouse stood, and behind us, where you see that sort of jungle-looking place, that was where the gardens began."

"His uncle has a movie of the gardens," Alan Mendelsohn said. "Whatever happened to them?"

"Well, this part of town started to get developed," Noel Wallaby said, "lots of cars and houses and factories —and airplanes flying overhead. They all created pollution, and a lot of the plants and trees, which were tropical and sort of delicate, just died. Then Mr. Hergeschleimer disappeared, and the place just sort of fell apart. You can still follow some of the paths, and some of the trees are still alive, though not at this time of the year. Do you boys want to go over the back fence and walk around?"

We did.

"OK, just be careful back there. If you get lost, holler

for Fafner. He'll come back there and lead you out. And be sure to be back by 1 P.M—that's when I close on Saturdays."

Alan Mendelsohn and I climbed over the fence at the back of the junkyard and into the ruins of Hergeschleimer's Oriental Gardens. Just after the fence there were a lot of beaten-up bushes and garbage, tall grass and dead weeds. We had a little trouble crashing through all that. Then things opened up a bit, although the grass and weeds were still pretty high. We found a gravel path and followed it.

"This must have been great once," Alan Mendelsohn said.

We followed the path through avenues of huge trees. Some of the trees were dead, and some of them had fallen. A few lay across the path, and we had to scramble over them. We came upon little clearings. In one of them a stone statue of a Buddha was almost hidden by weeds. We found a little lake where a few wild geese that still hadn't flown south were swimming.

We went a long way. The noise of cars on Utopia Avenue was far behind us, barely heard.

We really liked Hergeschleimer's Oriental Gardens—or what remained of them. For a while, we actually forgot all about what we had come for, all about making contact with a parallel plane of existence. The ruined gardens were so interesting that we just wanted to walk around and enjoy them. We sat on a big rock and watched the Canada geese for a long time.

"Well, we're here," I said.

"Yeah," Alan Mendelsohn said.

"This is supposed to be a place where we can make contact with another plane of existence," I said.

"If we go into state twenty-six," Alan Mendelsohn said.

"Yeah," I said.

"Well, do you want to do it?"

"We might as well—I mean, that's what we came here for."

"Do you want to do this one at a time, so the other one can sort of watch out for you, or both at once?"

I thought it over. "Both at once," I said.

We closed our eyes and went into state twenty-six. When we opened our eyes, everything was the same. We were still sitting on that same rock, the geese were still swimming around in the little lake. The trees rustled over our heads.

"Nothing happened?" I said.

"No. Well, maybe. I mean, I'm not sure," Alan Mendelsohn said.

I knew what he meant. Everything was the same—but it wasn't. I don't know exactly what we expected. I wasn't sure if I felt anything out of the ordinary. It seemed awfully quiet.

There was something different about the light. It was sort of pink. The geese were the same geese we'd been watching before we went into state twenty-six, but there was something special about them now. They were—this is hard to explain—more real.

"Are you in state twenty-six now?" Alan Mendelsohn asked.

"I'm not sure. Are you?"

"I can't tell either."

We sat on the rock for a few minutes—it seemed like a long time. Both of us were trying to sense if anything had happened. Finally, Alan Mendelsohn spoke.

"There shouldn't be so many leaves on the trees at this time of year," he said.

"And they shouldn't be green," I said.

"Can you see leaves on the trees?" Alan Mendelsohn asked.

"Yes. No. I mean, yes and no. I can see the leaves, and I can see the trees bare—both at the same time."

"Yeah, me too," Alan Mendelsohn said. "Do those geese look different to you?"

"Yes and no."

"That's right," Alan Mendelsohn said. "I feel weird. I

feel split up. It's like I'm in two places at once—one as real as the other."

"That's how I feel too," I said. "I'm in a place that's cold and a place that's warm—and they're both this place."

"That's it!" Alan Mendelsohn said. "That's why there are certain places where you can make contact with parallel planes! This place exists in both planes! Or there are two places just alike, one on top of the other, and both in the same spot. We've done it! We're in touch with a parallel existential plane!"

"Do you really think so?" I asked. This was getting exciting.

"It has to be," Alan Mendelsohn said. "How else could we be cold and warm? How else could the trees be bare and leafy? And what in the world is the Mad Guru doing here?"

35

It was true. There he was, the Mad Guru, the guy who hung out in William Lloyd Floyd's bookstore, picking his way through the underbrush.

"Well, well," the Mad Guru said as he approached us, "Where in Waka-Waka did you two come from?"

We had both realized by this time that the Mad Guru was not visible in both the almost identical worlds we could see. This may be hard to understand, but we were both getting used to looking at two worlds at once. It was as though someone had drawn a picture of a tree in winter on a piece of thin paper, and then traced the picture of the tree and added leaves—as if it were summer. Then, imagine holding one picture over the other—but not exactly lined up—and holding them both up to the light. We could see the ruins of Hergeschleimer's Oriental Gardens in winter—which was what we would have expected to see—and at the same time, we could see Hergeschleimer's Oriental Gardens in full summer foliage. We could see these things at the same time, and we could see both of them separately. It was confusing—but not as confusing as you might think. It was like looking at one thing and listening to another at the same time.

What was surprising about the Mad Guru was that he was in the summertime picture—the parallel plane of existence—not in our everyday world where we were used to seeing him.

"What are you doing here?" we both asked at once.

"That's what I asked you," the Mad Guru said. "I don't recall ever seeing you before."

"Sure you have," Alan Mendelsohn said. "We met you at William Lloyd Floyd's bookstore. We had lunch together. And we met in the street once; and then we saw you when I sold my comic books."

"Are you sure?" the Mad Guru asked. "I think you may have gotten me mixed up with somebody else."

"Aren't you the Mad Guru?" I asked.

"No. My brother Arnie is the Mad Guru. My name is Lance Hergeschleimer."

"Wait a minute," Alan Mendelsohn said. "Are you the Lance Hergeschleimer who used to own Hergeschleimer's Oriental Gardens?"

"I still own them," the man said.

"And disappeared a long time ago?" Alan Mendelsohn went on.

"Do I look as if I had disappeared?" the man said. "Although I suppose when you go from one place, or plane, to another, you could be said to have disappeared from the place where you used to be. But, one never thinks of oneself as having disappeared, because one is always right there, if you know what I mean. I didn't disappear so much as leave. What I did was leave the city of Hogboro, in the United States of America, in whatever plane of reality those places exist, to come and live here in Waka-Waka, just as you have."

"This is Waka-Waka?" I asked.

"It is," Lance Hergeschleimer said.

"And you came here?" Alan Mendelsohn asked.

"I did."

"How?"

"State twenty-six, same as anybody who comes to live here—same as you."

"But we thought we were the first Earth people ever to attain state twenty-six by our own will," Alan Mendelsohn said.

"Nonsense," Lance Hergeschleimer said. "Where'd you get a strange idea like that?"

"Clarence Yojimbo. . . ."

"Clarence Yojimbo, the Venusian hippie?" Lance Hergeschleimer exclaimed. "He's madder than my brother Arnie! He was here a few months ago with a bunch of eight-hundred-year-old men on motorcycles—folk singers they were. He's wrong about state twenty-six. That's how I got here. That's how lots of people get here who want to live in Waka-Waka instead of their old world."

"We didn't come to live here," I said. I was getting a little nervous.

"Of course you did, boy," Lance Hergeschleimer said. "Nobody ever goes back."

This worried me quite a bit. I hadn't counted on going to live in Waka-Waka. I didn't even know if I liked it. And besides, there were my parents, and Melvin, the dog, and Grandfather and the Old One. They wouldn't know where I was.

Obviously, Alan Mendelsohn was worried too, by Lance Hergeschleimer's insistence that nobody ever goes back. "Mr. Hergeschleimer," he asked, "is it warm or cold?"

"Why, it's warm," Lance Hergeschleimer said. "It's always warm, or at least mild, in Waka-Waka."

"Do you see any leaves on the trees?" I asked.

"Excuse me, young fellows, but I think you're asking me silly questions," Lance Hergeschleimer said. "Is there any point to all this?"

"Yes there is," Alan Mendelsohn said. "We'll explain in a moment, but first please answer the question. Do the trees have leaves?"

"Of course the trees have leaves," Lance Hergeschleimer said impatiently. "It's the middle of summer. It's been the middle of summer for twenty-five years—that's how the seasons are here. Every tree has leaves."

"None of them are bare?" I asked.

"Not one," Lance Hergeschleimer said. "Now what's this all about?"

"One more question," Alan Mendelsohn said. "Hogboro—the place you used to live—can you see it now?"

"Certainly not," Lance Hergeschleimer said. "I'm here, not there."

"Well, you see, Mr. Hergeschleimer," Alan Mendelsohn said, "I think Leonard and I—by the way, this is my friend, Leonard Neeble, and I am Alan Mendelsohn. . . ."

"Glad to meet you," Lance Hergeschleimer said.

". . . I think that we are here *and* there. I'll explain. Right now, it's the beginning of winter in Hogboro. All the leaves have fallen. The trees are bare. The weather is fairly cold. We can see and feel that. At the same time, we can see and feel summer in Waka-Waka. We can see you—but only in the Waka-Waka summer. In the Hogboro winter, you do not exist."

"Well! If that is true, it's really something out of the ordinary!" Lance Hergeschleimer said. "I thought only extraterrestrials could go back and forth between planes like that. My goodness!"

"Well, that's how it is," Alan Mendelsohn said.

"If that's the case, I'll bet you could take a message to my brother Arnie, the Mad Guru," Lance Hergeschleimer said. "He's probably still wondering what happened to me. But you'll be wanting to learn more about Waka-Waka—it's an ideal society."

I was just getting ready to ask Lance Hergeschleimer some questions about the ideal society of Waka-Waka, when he suddenly grabbed Alan Mendelsohn and me by the shoulders, and pushed us down behind a bush. "Duck! Duck!" Lance Hergeschleimer said. "And don't make a sound if you value your lives!"

Lance Hergeschleimer crouched with us behind the bush. He was sweating. It was easy to see that he was really scared. Alan Mendelsohn and I were scared too. We couldn't see or hear anything out of the ordinary.

We wondered what it was that Lance Hergeschleimer
had noticed to frighten him so.

After a while, Lance Hergeschleimer seemed to relax.
"That was a close one," he sighed.

"A close one?" I asked.

"A close call," Lance Hergeschleimer said. "It almost
got us that time."

"What did?" Alan Mendelsohn asked.

"What did?" Lance Hergeschleimer repeated. "The
thing without a name—the accursed thing—the unspeakable awfulness. It does *their* bidding."

"*Their* bidding? Who are *they*?" Alan Mendelsohn asked.

"Not now, boy—I'll explain it later," Lance Hergeschleimer said, raising one finger.

"But Mr. Hergeschleimer," I said, "I didn't see or
hear anything."

"Then it's lucky you were with me," Lance Hergeschleimer said. "I'm especially good at sensing the presence of the unseen attacker—the invisible antagonist—the
ineffable ickiness. I know when it's near. That's why I
can walk around like this, in the open, with relative
safety. You boys are all right as long as you're with me.
When I say duck—you duck."

"Wait a minute," Alan Mendelsohn said. "What exactly
is this terrible monster?"

"That's good," Lance Hergeschleimer said, "the terrible monster—the terrific molester—the terrorist man-
gler—that's very good."

"Well, what's it all about?" I asked, "and who are
they?"

"I told you—later," Lance Hergeschleimer said. "Now I
can continue to show you around the ideal society without trouble—the intangible trouncer seldom appears more
than once in a day."

"Some ideal society," Alan Mendelsohn whispered to
me.

Lance Hergeschleimer overheard him. "Everything is

relative," he said. "When you've seen the benefits of Waka-Waka, you'll realize that the unexampled eviscerator is a minor inconvenience by comparison."

"This I've got to see," Alan Mendelsohn said, and we followed Lance Hergeschleimer through the Oriental Gardens which bore his name.

36

Lance Hergeschleimer led us along the paths of Hergeschleimer's Oriental Gardens, back toward the junkyard. When we got to the tangled bushes and the wire fence, we ran into a little trouble.

While we were inside the gardens, the matter of being in two places—or existential planes—at once wasn't too difficult. After all, it was the same place in both worlds, and all we had to deal with was two versions—two seasons, really—of Hergeschleimer's Oriental Gardens, sort of superimposed. From the edge of the Gardens, we could see two *different* worlds, and that was altogether another sort of thing.

We could see the junkyard and the little shack where Noel Wallaby stayed, but in more or less the same place was the big teahouse, the one we had seen glimpses of in Uncle Boris's film, the one that didn't exist anymore—in our world. There was the highway—and there was a big Vaka-Wakian forest, growing right through the highway. There was a sort of path through the forest, which ran right through Noel Wallaby's shack, which seemed just as solid as the Waka-Wakian trees around it. I felt—well, sort of carsick, dizzy.

"Right this way, boys," Lance Hergeschleimer said.

If we had followed him, we would have had to walk through the solid walls of Noel Wallaby's junkyard shack and then out into the highway, where solid cars would mow us down.

"Just a minute, Mr. Hergeschleimer," Alan Mendelsohn said. "We have a little problem here."

"What do you suppose we ought to do?" I asked.

"I'm not sure," Alan Mendelsohn said.

He touched the wire fence which existed only in the Hogboro plane. Then he touched a wooden railing that existed only in the Waka-Waka plane. "They're both solid," he said.

"Do you realize something?" I asked.

"What?"

"We're not in two existential planes at once—we're trapped *between* two existential planes."

"This may be serious," Alan Mendelsohn said.

"What seems to be the trouble?" Lance Hergeschleimer wanted to know.

We explained it to him.

"That really is a problem," Lance Hergeschleimer said. "Under ordinary circumstances, we don't feel, see, hear, smell, or taste anything from another plane of existence—maybe once in a while we get a sort of faint impression, but that's all. Still, at the same time, activity in the other planes is going on all around, and even through us. When you boys came here, you probably walked right through Waka-Wakian trees and buildings, and didn't even know it. Now, everything feels solid, am I right?"

"Yes," Alan Mendelsohn said. "What do you think we should do?"

"I haven't the faintest idea," Lance Hergeschleimer said. "Of course, you two seem to be especially good at state twenty-six. Maybe you could try using it to work this problem out—if not, I'll have to say good-bye. can't be late for lunch, and we don't have very much time."

It was certainly worth a try. We didn't like the idea of being left by Lance Hergeschleimer, trapped between two existential planes—and the accursed thing, or whatever it was, apt to turn up at any moment. We went into state twenty-six and experimented with the solidity of

objects. It didn't take very long to get results. We found
we could tune ourselves like the fine-tuning knob on a
television set. We could tune Waka-Waka down until it
was almost invisible—just like a ghost in a TV picture.
When we did that, the Waka-Waka wooden railing, which
could hardly be seen, was as insubstantial as air. When
we tuned down Hogboro, the wire fence gradually dis-
solved, until it was just a vague smudge before our eyes,
and then we could pass our hands right through it. It
took a few minutes to get used to doing this. Then Alan
Mendelsohn thought of something.

"Mr. Hergeschleimer, when we tune out Waka-Waka,
do we become invisible?"

"I was just remarking to myself about that," Lance
Hergeschleimer said. "You don't become entirely invisible—if I try real hard, I can just make out your outlines
—but if I wasn't sure you were there, I'd pay no attention to you. You just become sort of thick places in the
air."

"This may come in handy later," Alan Mendelsohn
said to me.

We surprised Noel Wallaby by appearing and vanishing
before his eyes. When we invisibly left his junkyard, he
was cleaning his eyeglasses with the tail of his shirt and
talking excitedly to his dog, Fafner.

The forest through which Alan Mendelsohn and I
followed Lance Hergeschleimer was not open and parklike,
like Hergeschleimer's Oriental Gardens. It was sort of
dark. The trees were tall and grew close together. The
forest floor was all tangled roots and rotten leaves, and
wherever there was dirt it was black and slippery and
smelled funny. There was a cold wind blowing through
the forest. Sometimes it was so dark we could hardly see
where to put our feet. I fell down a few times, and so did
Alan Mendelsohn.

"This place is called Moo-Shu Forest," Lance Hergeschleimer said. "It got its name from a Chinese restaurant
that existed here a long time ago. Nobody remem-

bers the name of the Chinese restaurant, but Moo-Shu pork was one of the dishes they served there."

"There was a Chinese restaurant in the middle of a forest?" Alan Mendelsohn asked.

"Oh, there's quite a bit in this forest, as you'll see later on," Lance Hergeschleimer said. "It's a nice place, really; cool in summer, easy to hide in, and the dreadful destroyer doesn't come here very often—it doesn't like dim places, just bright sun and . . . total darkness." When Lance Hergeschleimer said the word *darkness*, he sort of shuddered.

"About this dreadful destroyer," I said.

"Yes, the demon of darkness," Lance Hergeschleimer interrupted. "I'd prefer that we not discuss that particular topic right now—later, if you don't mind."

"Well, will you tell us this," Alan Mendelsohn asked. "Does everybody live out here in the woods? Don't you have any cities?"

"Oh ho. Ha ha. Hoo hoo," Lance Hergeschleimer said. "Don't we have any cities? Hee hee. Hoo hah. Ho ho." He didn't sound as though he was laughing—he just said the words *ho ho*, and so forth. "We have a city. We have the greatest city in this or any other world. We have a city—Lenny. Lenny the great. Lenny the rich. Lenny the beautiful."

"The city is named Lenny?" I asked.

"Yes," Lance Hergeschleimer said. "You think that's funny? You think that's a funny name for a city? And I suppose you think Chicago is a pretty name. Lenny is the name of our great city. It is named after the bravest man ever to live in Waka-Waka."

"Are you taking us to the city? To Lenny?" I asked.

"Well, actually, almost nobody ever goes to Lenny anymore—unless they have to. People live—sort of—in the suburbs now."

"Well, where are you taking us?" Alan Mendelsohn asked.

"I'm taking you to my cave," Lance Hergeschleimer

said. "I share a cave with a lot of other people. They're very nice—you'll see. We're almost there now."

For some time I had been pretty sure that pairs of eyes were watching us through the heavy underbrush. Once or twice I thought I saw someone—or something— darting through the forest ahead of us. This had me worried, until Lance Hergeschleimer told us that the dismal dreadfulness, or whatever they called it, didn't like the forest. But someone was watching us. I was sure of that when I saw Lance Hergeschleimer disappear into a pit someone had dug in the forest path and then carefully covered with leaves.

37

"Let me out! Let me out!" Lance Hergeschleimer shouted. "It's me, you fools! It's Lance Hergeschleimer!"

There wasn't a sound in the forest—other than Lance Hergeschleimer's shouting. Alan Mendelsohn and I stepped, carefully, closer to the edge of the pit.

"Are you boys still up there?" Lance Hergeschleimer was sitting in a puddle of muddy water, about ten feet down. "Stand where they can see you," he said. "If they just hear me shouting, they may think it's the horrendous horror trying to trick them."

We stood around, not too close to the edge of the pit. Without a rope, there was no way to get Lance Hergeschleimer out.

"It's me!" he shouted, every few minutes. "They'll be along soon," he said to us. "They're watching.—Just as soon as they're sure this isn't a trick, they'll come and get me out. It's this one fellow, Eugene, you see—he keeps setting traps for the maniacal marauder, and then forgetting to tell the rest of us where they are. I've been caught this way five or six times—we all have. Once, I was caught in a rope snare, and dangled from a tree by my right foot for half an hour. It's me! It's Lance Hergeschleimer, your friend! Get me out of here, you imbeciles!"

We stood around, feeling sort of useless and a little scared, while Lance Hergeschleimer bellowed from the bottom of the pit.

"What do we do if the horrible you-know-what turns up?" I whispered to Alan Mendelsohn.

"Well," he whispered back, "if the thing doesn't take us totally by surprise, I suppose the best thing to do would be to go into state twenty-six and tune ourselves back to the Hogboro plane. If it doesn't turn out that we're standing in the middle of a highway, that should get us away from here safely."

We heard a rustling in the bushes, got scared, and involuntarily went half-invisible, before we saw that the noise was caused by a bunch of ordinary-looking people carrying a long ladder. They lowered the ladder into Lance Hergeschleimer's pit, and he clambered out.

"Well, you certainly took your time!" Lance Hergeschleimer said.

"We had to be sure it was you, Lance," one of the people who had brought the ladder said. "We had to be sure it wasn't the dreadful dreariness, trying to trick us."

Lance Hergeschleimer looked at us. "See? What did I tell you?" He was trying to brush off his trousers, which were hopelessly muddy. "At least, no harm was done—thanks for asking," he said, "but I've forgotten to introduce our guests. Leonard and Alan, these are the people I live with—my cave-mates." Then Lance Hergeschleimer reeled off a bunch of names. I hate it when people do that—I can never remember who is who. I caught a few names: Clara, Walter, Helena, Raymond—but the only name I was able to connect with a person was Eugene. He was the guy who had dug the pit that Lance Hergeschleimer had fallen into. Eugene looked embarrassed.

After Lance Hergeschleimer had introduced us to everybody—and, except for Eugene, I didn't have any idea of who was who—the group of people led us off to their cave, which wasn't far away. As we walked, Lance Hergeschleimer's cave-mates all fussed about the fact that, at the time of his falling into the pit and making a commotion, he was already seven minutes late for lunch, and everyone was getting very upset. They went on and on about this—how Lance Hergeschleimer was late for lunch, and how they didn't know what to do, and how there were now two extra people to feed, and luckily there was enough food, but what if there hadn't been—and on and on and on.

Each person repeated the whole thing about how Lance Hergeschleimer had been seven minutes late, and how this upset everyone—and then they'd repeat it again. It was about the dumbest thing I'd ever heard. Nobody paid any attention to Alan Mendelsohn and me. We just walked along with this gang of complaining people because there wasn't any place to go, short of giving up on the whole adventure and going back to the Hogboro plane.

The cave itself was sort of neat. You had to crawl through a narrow, low, tunnellike doorway, and then you were in a very big room carved out of solid rock. Opening off the big central room were little rooms, or sets of rooms—the apartments where the people who shared the cave lived. The central room had a big table, all set for lunch. There must have been places for twenty or thirty people.

Everybody went straight to the table, carrying on all the time about lunch having never been this late before, and how they hoped nothing was spoiled. Nothing was, it turned out, but you couldn't have told from my experience. It was, without a doubt, the worst-tasting food I've ever eaten. They served something that looked like a dead alley cat, and tasted worse. It turned out to be made of roots and bark. Now, with my grandmother being who she is, I've had a lot of experience with weird-tasting food—so when I say that this dead alley cat made of roots and bark tasted terrible, I mean terrible! There were a few other things, but I didn't even try them. Alan Mendelsohn tasted a couple of the other dishes and said the dead alley cat was the best part of the meal. Lance

Hergeschleimer and his friends ate just as though everything was all right.

At the end of the meal, Lance Hergeschleimer told us that because they had guests, the cave people were going to serve a special treat—a drink called fleegix. Alan Mendelsohn and I were interested in that, because we'd heard of fleegix before—once when Samuel Klugarsh was telling us about the Martian High Commissioner, Rolzup, and once when Clarence Yojimbo mentioned it to us.

"Isn't fleegix sort of like hot chocolate?" I asked Lance Hergeschleimer.

"Only much, much better," he said, "but where did you ever hear about fleegix?"

We told him about Clarence Yojimbo and the Martian High Commissioner.

"Do you know Rolzup?" Lance Hergeschleimer asked.

"No," I said, "we just heard about him—why?"

"Because he's coming here," Lance Hergeschleimer said, "in response to our urgent plea for help in dealing with *them* and the unapparent antagonist."

"Really?" Alan Mendelsohn asked. "Could we meet him?" He was really excited. I never knew he was so interested in meeting celebrities.

I had a question of my own, which just couldn't wait any longer. "Who," I asked Lance Hergeschleimer, "are *they*, and what is this unseen thing you're all so scared of."

"Yes," Lance Hergeschleimer said, "I did promise to tell you about the situation with *them* and *it*. Now is a good time to tell the whole story without interruption. While the fleegix is being prepared, I'll tell you everything."

38

"Civilization in Waka-Waka is very old," Lance Hergeschleimer said, "much older than it is in the plane of existence from which we came—the world which contains Hogboro. A long time ago, all the problems which afflict your world were solved here. People learned to get along without war, crime, and confusion. Also, all problems of survival were solved a long time ago. There were food and fleegix enough for everyone. Everyone understood his role in society, and everyone was content. For a long time, once things had progressed to the point where nobody had to work for a living, there was intense activity in the arts.

"That was the period during which our great city, Lenny, was built and adorned. Wonderful buildings were designed and constructed; people worked to make beautiful paintings and sculpture; works of music involving thousands of fine musicians were composed and performed every day. Science and engineering also flourished, and everything imaginable was done to make life a pure pleasure.

"This went on for a very long time—so long that nobody can quite remember how long. After a while, it seemed that everything that could possibly be done, had been done—and the happy people of Waka-Waka left off creating new pleasures, and settled down to enjoy the ones they already had.

"Little by little, the people forgot how to make amazing buildings, how to paint pictures, make statues, compose music—but it didn't matter, because there was already so much to enjoy in those areas.

"So the people became specialists in enjoying the fine things they already had. Everyone spent most of the time quietly admiring the great accomplishments of Waka-Waka's splendid past.

"Little by little, people began to lose interest in the buildings, the paintings, the music, and so forth. The people having learned to truly appreciate aesthetic experiences, the experiences themselves got smaller and smaller. People were satisfied to spend a whole day looking at a single flower, or even a weed, and maybe drinking a cup of fleegix. Little by little, the thing of beauty they were experiencing grew less and less important; the important thing was the ritual of experiencing it—and the cup of fleegix.

"Finally, the whole cultural life of Waka-Waka was based on drinking fleegix. Since there had been no political life or economic life for a long time—and Waka-Wakians never had much in the way of religion—there wasn't really anything to do but enjoy the drinking of fleegix."

Alan Mendelsohn interrupted. "You mean, that's all you do—just sit around and drink fleegix?"

"Oh, it's hard to understand if you haven't really experienced it fully," Lance Hergeschleimer said. "It isn't just sitting around and sipping something hot—although that's part of it. You see, all the experience of life has been, as it were, boiled down to fleegix drinking. Contained within the subtle and complicated ritual of drinking fleegix is all that is, or ever was, good or beautiful in the life of Waka-Waka. It's like baseball, television, art museums, and presidential elections, all rolled into one. It's all a Waka-Wakian needs to be happy.

"Now, I said that Waka-Waka had no political or economic life. That isn't precisely true—the one industry that flourished after everything else was finished was the manufacturing of fleegix, and the making of beautiful cups and other things used in the fleegix drinking ceremony. We also exported fleegix to some other planes of existence in which fleegix is popular—although nothing like it is here. Our main customer was the twelfth existential plane on Mars, where they like fleegix very much. In return for the fleegix we exported, the Martians would send us the little plant called *Zigismunda formosa*. We encase these little plants in the Lucite handles of our fleegix cups—it's a very important part of the fleegix ritual. It's a sort of holdover from the days when Waka-Wakians liked to spend the whole day looking at a flower or a weed while drinking their fleegix."

"Excuse me, Mr. Hergeschleimer," I said, "this is very . . . well, sort of . . . interesting—but I thought you were going to tell us about *them* and *it*."

"I was just coming to that," Lance Hergeschleimer said. "After nobody knows how many hundreds of years of living in perfect peace and tranquility, enjoying good relations with our neighbors, our life was totally uprooted by *them*.

"First, I have to explain to you that our great city, Lenny, is built on the sides of a mountain. The city goes almost to the top—in fact, the city looks like a mountain made of buildings. At the very top of the mountain-city grows a variety of bush found nowhere else in Waka-Waka. It is called the zitzkis, and it produces a berry which is utterly essential to the successful making of fleegix.

"There are only four zitzkis bushes, and each of them bears only a few berries each year—but one berry can impart its special flavor to over six thousand pounds of unbrewed fleegix. The zitzkis bush, as I mentioned, grows nowhere else but the summit of the mountain-city of Lenny. It can't be cultivated—it just grows wild. During the period of artistic and scientific activity in Waka-Waka, our chemists did practically nothing but try to find a synthetic substitute for the zitzkis berry. Without it, fleegix smells and tastes like spoiled fish. The attempts to find a substitute for the zitzkis berry failed. The best synthetic fleegix tasted like month-old flat root beer. All of Waka-Waka depended on those four bushes at the summit of Lenny.

"Then *they* came and took over: first the top of the mountain, where our zitzkis bushes grow—then they took over the top half of the city of Lenny—and finally, the whole thing. And of course, they have *it*, the unspeakable beast, to do their bidding and terrorize the people. That's why we all moved out of Lenny and into the forest."

"But who *are* they, and what *is* it?" Alan Mendelsohn and I shouted.

"Yes, yes, I'm coming to that," Lance Hergeschleimer said. "But I see that our fleegix is ready. Let's stop for now and enjoy it. I need to calm down a bit before telling you the rest of the story."

39

The fleegix tasted lousy. I wasn't surprised. It tasted worse than the watery hot chocolate my mother makes. The stuff they serve at the Bermuda Triangle Chili Parlor is ten thousand times better.

Lance Hergeschleimer and his friends made a big deal about drinking the fleegix. This didn't surprise me either. After all, from what Lance Hergeschleimer had just told us, it was all they had in the way of entertainment. Nobody made a sound while they handed around the cups of fleegix. The cups were made of plastic. They were like some cups my parents have for drinking coffee and stuff outdoors—they're called thermo-cups, or something like that, and they have double walls, with an air space between—they're supposed to keep your drink hot longer than an ordinary cup. It doesn't work. The handles of the cups were made of transparent plastic, and inside each handle was a little sprig of weed. I supposed that was the *Zigismunda formosa* Lance Hergeschleimer had told us about.

Once the cups of fleegix were distributed (they were about one-third full, which I wasn't sorry about) everybody sat around with closed eyes, taking a little sip now and then. I tried to get into it, closing my eyes and taking little sips—but it just tasted like watery hot chocolate to me. I could see that Alan Mendelsohn wasn't too excited by the fleegix either. The fleegix-drinking ceremony went on and on. It seemed like it was going to last forever.

Since everybody's eyes were closed, it seemed like it might be a good time to slip away and have a private conversation with Alan Mendelsohn. I poked him in the ribs and held up two fingers, and then six. Alan Mendelsohn nodded, and we both went into state twenty-six, and tuned ourselves out of the Waka-waka plane and back to Hogboro. It turned out we were sitting in the front yard of a house in West Kangaroo Park—about six blocks from where I lived.

"What do you think?" I asked Alan Mendelsohn.

"About the doings in Waka-Waka?" he asked. "So far, I'm really sorry that I sold my comic books. Still, I'd like to hear about *them* and *it*, if Lance Hergeschleimer ever finishes his story; and I would like to meet Rolzup, if we get the chance."

"But mostly, it is sort of boring," I said.

"For sure," Alan Mendelsohn said. "It *would* be our luck that we get to visit another plane of existence, and it turns out to be the dullest place in creation—and that fleegix—yuck!"

"Well, let's give it a few more hours," I said. "It's still early, and things may pick up."

"Sure," Alan Mendelsohn said. "I've got nothing else to do—and besides, I've got an idea we may be able to help those dullards out with their problem. They're not mean or evil—just *so* uninteresting."

We tuned ourselves back to Waka-Waka. Everybody was still sitting around contemplating their fleegix. I guessed that the whole business took half an hour.

Finally, the Waka-Wakians started to wake up, and blink, and look around. They all looked very contented.

"There!" Lance Hergeschleimer said. "Wasn't that beautiful?"

"Oh, yes—beautiful," Alan Mendelsohn and I said.

"I'm glad we had a little fleegix on hand so you could have this rich experience," Lance Hergeschleimer said. "*They* only gave us enough so that we don't go crazy and revolt. Often we don't have any fleegix for days at a time."

The other Waka-Wakian cave people were drifting away, cleaning up the fleegix things, and wandering off to their little rooms.

"Mr. Hergeschleimer," I said, "about *them*—you were going to tell us about *them* and *it*."

"Oh, yes," Lance Hergeschleimer said. "I was so transported from ugly reality by the fleegix experience that it completely slipped my mind. Thanks for reminding me." Then he fell silent.

"Yes?" Alan Mendelsohn said.

"Yes?" answered Lance Hergeschleimer.

"About *them*," I reminded him.

"Oh, yes. *Them*. Where did I leave off?"

I hoped this was going to be worth the effort. "They came," I said, "and took over the zitzkis bushes and half the city of Lenny, and then *they* kicked everybody out of the city of Lenny. Who are *they*?"

"*They*," said Lance Hergeschleimer, "are three Nafsulian freebooters—pirates, plunderers—known as Manny, Moe and Jack. Somehow they managed to cross the interplanar barrier, just as you did. Upon arriving here they looked around for our most valuable commodity to steal. Naturally, in our fleegix culture, the most valuable things we have are the zitzkis bushes, so they took those over. Since they couldn't take them away with them, they stayed here and set up a sort of pirate empire. They export our zitzkis berries at cutthroat prices, and give us just enough berries to make a tiny quantity of fleegix for our own use."

"But if there are only three of them, why didn't you all just kick them out?" Alan Mendelsohn asked.

"Well, my boy," Lance Hergeschleimer said, "we can't do that for two reasons—first, we have such a highly evolved and peaceful civilization, that it's been centuries and centuries since we had any sort of police or army or tough guys. There's nobody here who would know just how to go about kicking them out. They're very scary,

you know. Second, they have *it*—the unspeakable beast
—the hateful thing—the malicious monster—The Wozzle."

"The Wozzle?"

"That's its proper name," Lance Hergeschleimer said.
"We're so scared of it, we don't even like to say the
word. Oh, it's a fearful thing, boys, and invisible. You
never know when it's lurking about, ready to bite, and
scratch, and thump you to death."

"Has it killed anybody recently?" Alan Mendelsohn
wanted to know.

"No, not lately," Lance Hergeschleimer said. "We've
learned to avoid it—to sense its presence—and we've
learned to stay in the dimly lit places, where it doesn't
like to come. At night, we hide in our caves."

"When was the last time it killed anybody?" Alan
Mendelsohn asked.

"Oh, a very long time ago," Lance Hergeschleimer
said. "I don't exactly remember when it was."

"Who did it kill?" Alan Mendelsohn asked.

"Who? Oh—somebody—I think—it was . . . actually,
I don't really remember who got killed," Lance Hergeschleimer said.

"I'd really like to know who got killed, and when,"
Alan Mendelsohn said. "Could you ask the others?"

Lance Hergeschleimer called out to his cave-mates,
who gradually straggled out of their little cells and gathered
in the big room. "I'm explaining to these newcomers
about . . . you know . . . *it*. . . ."

"The Wozzle," Alan Mendelsohn interrupted.

"Yes . . . that," Lance Hergeschleimer said. "Alan is
very much interested in knowing who the last person it
happened to kill might have been, and when this tragedy
took place. Will someone please tell him?"

There was a lot of confused muttering and arguing
among the cave people. It soon became clear that none
of them knew who The Wozzle had killed or when.

"Well, let me ask you this," Alan Mendelsohn said.

"When was the last time anyone has suffered any violence at all from The Wozzle, and who was it that was attacked?"

"I can answer that," Eugene said. "It was me. Not six years ago, I was standing on the edge of the forest, taking some sun, and something crept up behind me and gave me a terrible kick in the seat of the pants. It was the . . . you know . . . for sure, and it would have done worse, but I ran into the shadows, where it couldn't follow."

"Anyone else?" Alan Mendelsohn asked. There were no other firsthand experiences of The Wozzle. "Now, has anyone ever seen Manny, Moe and Jack?" Alan Mendelsohn asked.

"Oh, yes," Lance Hergeschleimer answered. "We've seen them many times. We see them when we have to go to the city of Lenny to collect our zitzkis berry rations—and sometimes they call us together and holler at us and frighten us."

"What do they look like?" Alan Mendelsohn asked.

"Oh, horrible!" Lance Hergeschleimer said. All the other cave dwellers nodded agreement. "They have mean faces, and they have strange, scary eyes. They're small, but wiry and hairy, and they have long, strange noses."

"Can anyone go to see them?" Alan Mendelsohn asked.

"Nobody would go to see them unless they're sent for," Lance Hergeschleimer said. "Why go looking for trouble?"

"When they do send for you, what happens?" Alan Mendelsohn asked.

"Well, first they sound this huge electric horn—you can hear it all over the countryside. That's our signal that they want us to come. Then we all gather on the steps of the Palace of Culture, the biggest building in the city. After a while, the three bandits come out and stand at the top of the steps, and call us names, and make faces at us. Then they go inside and send *it*. . . ."

"The Wozzle?"

"Yes, the . . . that thing, out to chase us away."

"What does The Wozzle do when it comes out?" Alan Mendelsohn asked.

"We don't wait to find out," Lance Hergeschleimer said. "The second they go inside, we all run away."

"This is very interesting, isn't it, Leonard?" Alan Mendelsohn said. "Now, tell us something about Nafsulia," he said to Lance Hergeschleimer.

"Well, there isn't much to tell," Lance Hergeschleimer said. "Nafsulia is all the things Waka-Waka is not. There's no order in Nafsulia, no culture, no government, no morality. We tried to contact some kind of government in Nafsulia, through our friend Rolzup, to see if we could get some help in stopping this tyranny—but Rolzup couldn't find any government in Nafsulia."

"Is Rolzup nearby?" Alan Mendelsohn wanted to know.

"Yes," Lance Hergeschleimer said.

"We may want to see him later," Alan Mendelsohn said, "but first, I'd like to have a talk with my friend, Leonard. If you'll excuse us, we'll go out into the forest for a while. When we come back, we may have an interesting proposition for you."

40

"What's this all about?" I asked Alan Mendelsohn, when we were out of the cave and in the forest.

"Do you feel like taking a chance?" Alan Mendelsohn asked me.

"What do you mean?"

"I've got a feeling about The Wozzle and the Nafsulian pirates, Manny, Moe, and Jack," he said. "I think we may be able to straighten out this whole thing for the Waka-Wakians—but if I'm wrong, there may be some danger. Are you interested?"

"Well . . . sure," I said, "anything to make this adventure a little more interesting."

"Great," Alan Mendelsohn said. "Now, we've got to work fast. I'd like to get this whole thing wound up today. First, let's find a patch of sun in this forest."

We found a spot where the sun was shining through the trees and making a bright place on the forest floor. Alan Mendelsohn stood in the middle of the patch of sunlight. "I'm going to tune back to Hogboro, count to thirty, and then rematerialize here," he said. "Keep your eyes on the spot, and after I come back, tell me exactly what you saw."

Alan Mendelsohn faded away, and I was alone in the forest—it was eerie. I counted to thirty in my head, and at the count of thirty, Alan Mendelsohn began to reappear in the sunny spot.

"How was that?" he asked.

"Just fine," I said. "You vanished and reappeared."

"Now," Alan Mendelsohn said, "I'm going to try the same thing while standing in the shadows. Watch closely."

Alan Mendelsohn stepped into a shady place, and faded, and returned.

"Well," he said, "what did you see this time?"

"You didn't vanish completely," I said. "I could sort of see your outline if I squinted a little."

"Just as I thought," Alan Mendelsohn said. "Now we know why The Wozzle doesn't like shadowy places. This invisibility thing only works in bright light or total darkness. Remember, in Hergeschleimer's Oriental Gardens? Lance Hergeschleimer said he could still see us when we tuned ourselves into the Hogboro plane—he said we were like thick places in the air."

"Does this mean that there are sort of ghost images of us walking around Hogboro," I asked, "and do you think that's permanent? I mean, when we go home, will there be ghosts of us here in Waka-Waka?"

"I think we aren't really altogether in either place," Alan Mendelsohn said. "When we get ready to go home, I think we have to go to Hergeschleimer's Oriental Gardens in order to get all the way back into the Hogboro plane—the same way we got here. We can't get totally into Waka-Waka because we really belong in the Hogboro plane."

"But Lance Hergeschleimer is from the Hogboro plane, and he's totally here, and he can't get back," I said.

"Yes," Alan Mendelsohn said, "and that worries me. I wouldn't want to get stuck here, with the stupid fleegix, and all that. Maybe Rolzup will be able to tell us something about that."

"Rolzup?" I asked.

"Yes, that's the next step," Alan Mendelsohn said. "I'm going to talk with Rolzup. He may help us. He and I are both Martians, after all."

That was one of the things I liked about Alan Mendelsohn—you never knew what he was going to come up with next.

We went back into the cave. Alan Mendelsohn asked Lance Hergeschleimer to call all his cave-mates together.

"Look," Alan Mendelsohn said, "if The Wozzle were taken care of, do you think you could handle Manny, Moe and Jack?"

"I don't know," Lance Hergeschleimer said. "Nafsulians are pretty tough. They never give up—even when they pretend to surrender, they still have a lot of fight left in them. There's only one way to be sure that a Nafsulian is finished."

"And what's that?" Alan Mendelsohn asked.

"Well, there's one ultimate Nafsulian gesture of surrender," Lance Hergeschleimer said. "If a Nafsulian removes and replaces his hat continuously, while rubbing his belly with a circular motion, that is a gesture of surrender which no Nafsulian can retract."

Alan Mendelsohn and I looked at each other. "I can just about promise you a complete, unconditional surrender if you will just cooperate," Alan Mendelsohn said. "Now, how many Waka-Wakians live in this forest?"

"Oh, I'd say about twenty thousand," Lance Hergeschleimer said.

"Can you spread a message to all of them?" Alan Mendelsohn asked.

"Yes, we could do that," Lance Hergeschleimer said.

"OK," Alan Mendelsohn said. "Tell everybody to get a piece of wood suitable for making a torch. When you hear the electric horn calling you to the city of Lenny, everybody has to turn up with a burning torch. Tell everybody to pick up the rottenest, smokiest wood they can find. Will you do it?"

"How do we know this will work?" Lance Hergeschleimer asked.

"Because Rolzup, the Martian High Commissioner, is

going to give my plan his full approval," Alan Mendelsohn said, "if someone will just take me to him now."

Apparently, I wasn't supposed to go with Alan Mendelsohn to see Rolzup. This bugged me a little bit. I thought he was carrying this bit about being a Martian too far. I would have liked to see the Martian High Commissioner too. As it was, Alan Mendelsohn was led off by Lance Hergeschleimer and some other Waka-Wakians to the cave where Rolzup was staying. The rest of the people from Lance Hergeschleimer's cave hurried off to spread the word through the forest. I kept myself busy collecting torch wood.

I was on my own for about an hour. After I got the torch wood collected, I tuned back to Hogboro, just to see what was happening. It wasn't any more interesting there, and besides, it was cold, so I tuned back to Waka-Waka and just hung around the cave.

Finally, I heard voices and people crashing through the undergrowth, and Alan Mendelsohn, Lance Hergeschleimer, Eugene, and some other Waka-Wakians came into view.

"It was interesting," Alan Mendelsohn said. "I learned a lot. I had a private audience with Rolzup. Nobody else was allowed in—so you wouldn't have been able to see him, if you'd come along." It was nice of Alan Mendelsohn to at least mention that. I got over feeling mad at him for not taking me with him.

"Rolzup is all for my plan, and he's going to help us. Also I found out something even more important," Alan Mendelsohn said. "If anybody comes to Waka-Waka and stays a certain number of hours—he gets stuck here."

"How many hours?" I asked.

"Rolzup isn't sure," Alan Mendelsohn said. "He's been here before and stayed up to eight hours—then you have to stay away for at least a year and sort of build up an immunity—so I guess we can figure that up to eight hours is safe—at least for Rolzup and me. I don't know if it's the same for an Earth person. Maybe you should go back now, and I'll try to bring off my plan without you."

"Why don't you cut out that Martian stuff?" I said. "This is no time for it."

"Thanks, Leonard," Alan Mendelsohn said. "You're a brave kid. We've been here for about five hours, so we'd better wind things up in a hurry so we can get home. By the way," Alan Mendelsohn smiled, "Rolzup and I took care of some personal business too."

The truth is, I hadn't always known what Alan Mendelsohn was talking about. Sometimes, I thought he was a little crazy—for example, with his business about being a Martian—but he was my friend, and I usually just went along with whatever he wanted to do.

"Now, here's the plan," Alan Mendelsohn said. "By this time everybody has got their torches and instructions. Right now, the word is spreading that Rolzup has approved my plan—they all respect him a lot. I think they'll go through with it. Even though they're frightened of Manny, Moe and Jack, the Nafsulian bandits, they're really sick and tired of getting pushed around and not having all the fleegix they want. I'm sure you realized that we can get Manny, Moe and Jack to make the Nafsulian gesture of surrender—taking off their hats and rubbing their bellies—by using Klugarsh Mind Control."

"Sure. I realized that," I said.

"Well, Rolzup says that once we get them to surrender, he can transport them out of here and back to their own existential plane."

"I thought if you stayed here more than eight hours, you couldn't get out."

"That's Martians and Earth people—Nafsulians can go anywhere," Alan Mendelsohn said. "All we have to do is get Manny, Moe and Jack to summon all the people of Waka-Waka to the city of Lenny—then we neutralize the Wozzle, get them to surrender by using Klugarsh Mind Control, and the whole thing is wrapped up."

"Wait a minute!" I said. "How are we going to do all

those things? How will we get them to summon all the people? And what if we can't get them to surrender by Klugarsh Mind Control? We don't know if it works on Nafsulians. And what if The Wozzle doesn't want to be neutralized?"

"If any of those things happen, we just have to tune ourselves back to the Hogboro plane, and never come back here again—because if I'm wrong about any of this, and any of the Waka-Wakians survive, they'll never get over being mad at us."

"Look," I said, "I think we'd better talk this over some more."

"There's no time," Alan Mendelsohn said. "We've only got three hours to get this done—then we have to get back to Hergeschleimer's Oriental Gardens to make the complete return to our own existential plane—and it's a good half hour walk to Lenny, so we'd better start moving right now."

41

As we walked through the forest, I wondered if maybe Alan Mendelsohn wasn't really seriously crazy. If it took us a half hour to get to the city of Lenny, then it was going to take at least that long for the Waka-Wakians to get there with their torches. (I still didn't know what the torches were for—maybe Alan Mendelsohn was planning to burn down the city.) That meant that we'd be alone in the city of Lenny with Manny, Moe and Jack, the Nafsulian bad guys, and their terrible beast for at least a half hour after the electric horn was sounded. This didn't make me feel too comfortable, especially since I didn't know what Alan Mendelsohn's plan was, and he apparently wasn't going to take the time to tell me.

Alan Mendelsohn had a little map Rolzup had sketched for him, and he was constantly checking it and looking for landmarks as we made our way cross-country toward the city of Lenny. He didn't seem to be interested in talking as we walked.

The city of Lenny was pretty impressive. Just as Lance Hergeschleimer had described it, it looked like a mountain made of buildings. There was a highway leading up to a gate, and after that, an incredibly long and wide flight of steps leading up to a big building that looked a little like the Hogboro Museum. Alan Mendelsohn and I stepped onto the road and walked up to the gate.

"Who goes there? Who trespasses on the city of Manny, Moe and Jack?" a voice boomed.

"Pay no attention," Alan Mendelsohn said. "It's a recording—Rolzup told me about it."

"Halt, Interlopers!" The voice was even louder.

"Still a recording," Alan Mendelsohn said. "Don't worry about it."

We started climbing up the steps.

"BEWARE! THIS IS YOUR LAST WARNING!" The voice was *really* loud.

"Pay no attention, and keep climbing," Alan Mendelsohn said. "It's just a mechanical burglar alarm to alert Manny, Moe and Jack that someone is coming."

Ahead and above us, I could see the doors of the big building slowly opening. I couldn't see any people.

"PREPARE TO DIE!" the voice said—louder yet.

"Let's go, Alan," I said. "It's obvious we aren't wanted here."

"Don't worry," Alan Mendelsohn said. "They're just trying to scare us."

"Well, it's working," I said.

"Look!" Alan Mendelsohn said, pointing. "Manny, Moe and Jack!"

Three little men appeared. None of them could have been taller than five feet. They all had thick horn-rimmed eyeglasses, and they were wearing plaid sport jackets. Except for their greenish color, they could have been anybody. They didn't look pleasant, but they didn't look especially scary.

"Who dares?" one of them shouted in a thin, squeaky voice. He cupped his hand in front of his straw snap-brim hat so he could see us—the sun was behind us.

"To violate," another of the three Nafsulians squeaked.

"The sacred city of Manny, Moe and Jack?" the third said.

Alan Mendelsohn's reply surprised me. "We are emissaries of the Martian High Commissioner Rolzup—here to discuss matters concerning the zitzkis berry trade."

"Oh, wait a minute," said one of the Nafsulians. They

went into a huddle. "You may approach," they said, "but no tricks—or we will send our pet out to deal with you."

We approached. "We have been sent to find out," Alan Mendelsohn said as we got near the top step, "why you are charging us twelve Martian klatchniks per zitzkis berry, while the People's Zitzkis Berry Collective of Waka-Waka is able to offer them for three Martian klatchniks apiece."

"What?" Manny, Moe and Jack shouted. "What's that you say? Three klatchniks? That's impossible! Unless . . . unless the Waka-Wakians have a secret store of zitzkis berries . . . unless they've been saving zitzkis berries out of the generous free gifts of zitzkis berries we present to them. Treachery! the ingrates are trying to undermine our enterprise! Sound the alarm!"

One of the Nafsulian pirates ran inside the big building and apparently threw a switch, because the loudest electric horn I ever heard began to sound. "It worked," Alan Mendelsohn whispered to me.

By this time we were already at the top of the stairs. The three Nafsulians had brought out chairs and set them in a circle on the wide, flat place in front of the building. There was also a little table with cups of fleegix. Ugh! I thought to myself.

"I am Manny," one of the Nafsulians said, "and this is Moe, and this is Jack. Kindly sit down and have a cup of fleegix with us. A large portion of the Waka-Wakian populace will soon be here, and this misunderstanding will be cleared up. I'm afraid the reason you were offered those zitzkis berries at such an unconventional price is that they are, or were, purloined zitzkis berries. The ones who offered them to you had no right to do so. We control all zitzkis berries in Waka-Waka and the universe, and we set the price. It will all be cleared up in a very short time."

We sat through our second fleegix ritual of the day. This one was more interesting, because at least we had the green Nafsulians to look at. It was also fortunate that the pirates had adopted the Waka-Waka fleegix ritual, because it meant a half hour during which we wouldn't have to answer any questions. I was afraid they would ask me something about the twelfth existential plane on Mars.

As it was, the fleegix ritual didn't last long enough. The Nafsulian pirates came out of their aesthetic trance before anyone from the forest had arrived with a flaming torch. Manny, Moe and Jack didn't come out of their period of fleegix contemplation all fuzzy-headed and peaceful, like the Waka-Wakians—they seemed sort of sharp and suspicious. "How is it that our usual contacts, Doldup and Weezup weren't sent with this message?" Moe wanted to know.

"Doldup and Weezup are on vacation," Alan Mendelsohn said.

"That's odd," Jack said. "I've never heard of a Martian official taking a vacation."

"I can see that you're a Martian," Manny said to Alan Mendelsohn, "but your colleague . . . I didn't catch the name. . . ."

"Leonard," I blurted out.

"Leonard?" Manny said. "That's not a very Martian-sounding name. He doesn't look like any Martian I've ever seen."

"He's from the seventh existential plane," Alan Mendelsohn said. "He's just with our department temporarily—sort of an exchange program."

"People from the seventh existential plane on Mars ought to have gills," Manny said, "since everything there is under water."

"Look!" Alan Mendelsohn shouted, and pointed to a column of smoke rising near the gate to the city.

42

"What's that?" said Manny.

"It's the Waka-Wakian peasants, bearing torches," said Moe.

"Why are they carrying torches?" asked Jack.

"Who cares?" Manny said. "It's probably some weak trick of theirs to distract us so we won't ask them who's been stealing our zitzkis berries. They can't do any harm with those torches—the city is made entirely of stone."

The Waka-Waka populace was arriving in large groups and gathering on the wide steps of the Palace of Culture. Each Waka-Wakian carried a burning, smoking torch.

When all the Waka-Wakians had gathered on the steps, the three Nafsulians addressed them. "Miserable citizens of Waka-Waka," they began, "it has come to our attention that some of you have been offering *our* zitzkis berries to our Martian neighbors at a reduced price. We want the ringleaders. We will give five zitzkis berries to anyone who comes forward with information."

"Phooey!" someone in the crowd shouted.

"Banana oil!" shouted another.

"Your grandmother's mustache!" someone else said.

The Waka-Wakians weren't particularly original in their insults, but they were showing a lot of courage. I felt sort of proud of them.

"We will not waste any more time," the Nafsulians said. "We have important Martian guests to attend to." It was Moe who said this. I was glad they hadn't figured out that we were fakes. They were so excited by our story of zitzkis berries being sold without their knowledge, that they didn't even try to find out if it was true or not. Alan Mendelsohn told me later that this is called the "big lie" technique. You start off with a whopper, and try to spring it on your victim all of a sudden—and he'll be too excited to do much thinking. It's like this: someone rushes in and shouts, "YOUR GRANDMOTHER'S HOUSE IS ON FIRE—COME AND SAVE HER!" You might be six blocks away when you realize that your grandmother lives in a mobile home in Nefesh Park, Florida. The Nafsulians were just too greedy to stop and think when someone told them that their stolen zitzkis berries were being stolen from them. They just reacted.

"If someone doesn't talk right now, we'll just go inside and send out our little pet. He'll take care of you—if you know what we mean." The Nafsulians all laughed nasty laughs.

This was going to be the test of Waka-Wakian courage. I knew that Alan Mendelsohn had passed the word not to run away, even if the unfathomable evilness was sent for—but I also knew that the Waka-Wakians were deathly afraid of the monster, and usually ran the moment the Nafsulians threatened them with it. There was a wave of terror that went through the crowd—it was noticeable—but nobody ran. They all wanted to run—you could feel that too.

"Anybody feel like talking?" the pirates said.

Nobody made a sound or said a word. They just stood there, holding their torches.

"All right—you've brought this on yourselves," the Nafsulians said. "And just for fun, we've pushed the button that electrically locks the city gate—this time you can't run away from our pet."

There were some whimpers of fear from the crowd. It's one thing to make up your mind not to run away from a dreadful monster—it's something else entirely to find out you have no choice in the matter.

"Last chance," the Nafsulians said.

The three Nafsulian bandits went inside the doors of the Palace of Culture. There were a few scattered screams from the crowd. I had been feeling so sorry for the frightened Waka-Wakians that I forgot all about the fact that I was standing not twenty feet from the door out of which the intolerable abomination was going to appear any moment. All of a sudden I remembered that. I also realized that I was so scared and excited that I probably wasn't going to be able to go into state twenty-six if things went wrong. There were, maybe, five terrible seconds—the Waka-Wakians' torches wavered—the thick, choking black smoke made the whole city seem as dim as the forest—my heart was pounding.

Then something appeared in the doorway! The Wozzle! I felt sick and scared. It was as big as three men—three little men. Wait a minute! The Wozzle was supposed to be invisible—and yet, I could see something. In the dim light caused by the smoke from the torches I could see that The Wozzle—the invisible terror—was actually Manny, Moe and Jack, the three Nafsulian bandits! *They* were The Wozzle!

The Waka-Wakian populace caught on just a few seconds after I did. First there was some giggling—then some loud laughter—then a deafening roar. Manny, Moe and Jack looked confused. Twenty thousand Waka-Wakians, who were supposed to be scared silly, were pointing at them and laughing.

"Now!" Alan Mendelsohn whispered in my ear, "while they're still confused! Let's command them to surrender!" I went into state twenty-six with Alan Mendelsohn, and we commanded the three Nafsulians to remove and replace their little straw hats continuously, while rubbing their bellies with a circular motion—the old Klugarsh Mind Control trick.

It worked! The Nafsulians gradually became more visible, looking at each other with amazed expressions, as they continued to rub their bellies and remove their hats in the classic Nafsulian gesture of complete surrender

The crowd was cheering. "THEY'VE SURRENDERED! THEY'VE SURRENDERED!" Then the crowd began to call for the Martian High Commissioner. "ROLZUP! ROLZUP!" they shouted. People stepped to the side to make a little path through the crowd, and up the steps came a very dignified-looking man. He was wearing a sort of green-and-white sweater, and black-and-white shoes with plaid socks.

"I am Rolzup, High Commissioner of the twelfth existential plane on Mars," the dignified man in the sweater said. "I am here to officially acknowledge that you have made the ultimate gesture of surrender—which no Nafsulian can ever retract—and to offer, as the representative of a neutral government, to provide you with safe conduct and *make sure* you get home." The Nafsulians looked as though they were afraid of Rolzup. "We'll be starting out for the Nafsulian plane of existence almost at once," he said. And then he said to us, "I'd start out for home without hesitating, if I were you. I don't think you can stay here safely for much more than an hour—you don't want to get stuck in Waka-Waka." Then he waved to the cheering crowd of Waka-Wakians, and he and the three Nafsulians faded and vanished before our eyes.

Lance Hergeschleimer rushed up to us. "You boys are great Waka-Wakian heroes!" he said. "We want to honor you, and also celebrate our return to complete liberty, with an all-night fleegix ceremony beginning in one hour." There was wild cheering from the crowd. You couldn't hear yourself think. Alan Mendelsohn and I went into state twenty-six and tuned ourselves back to Hogboro.

43

We were across the street from Bat Masterson Junior High School. Although we had tuned ourselves as far as we could back to the Hogboro plane, we could still hear the faint cheering of the Waka-Wakian crowd. "We're not entirely here," I said.

"No, we're not," Alan Mendelsohn said. "We have to get to Hergeschleimer's Oriental Gardens in under an hour, or we're going to wind up stuck between Waka-Waka and whatever plane Hogboro exists in—or worse."

"You mean, if we don't go to Hergeschleimer's Oriental Gardens, tune ourselves to Waka-Waka, and then tune ourselves back to Hogboro, we might wind up sort of fading into Waka-Waka and staying there?"

"It's a possibility," Alan Mendelsohn said.

"Well, let's go," I said. "I don't want to spend the rest of my life drinking fleegix."

It was a long walk to Hergeschleimer's Oriental Gardens. We could just do it in under an hour, if we went fast the whole way and didn't stop. Of course, we weren't sure if an hour was all we had—it was just an educated guess of Rolzup's—but we didn't feel like taking any chances. We started walking, and went as fast as we could, not talking, sweating.

When we arrived at Noel Wallaby's junkyard, he had gone home. The gate was locked. There was barbed wire at the top of the fence. Fafner was there, but he didn't seem so old and harmless as before. Also, he didn't seem to recognize us. I had the feeling that he'd bite us with as many teeth as he had, if we got inside the fence.

"Without getting inside the junkyard, there's no way to get inside Hergeschleimer's Oriental Gardens," I said.

"I know," Alan Mendelsohn said. "I'm trying to think." He was all out of breath from the fast walk.

"We're wasting valuable time," I said.

"I know," Alan Mendelsohn said. "There's a way to get in there, but I can't think of it."

"Wait a minute!" I shouted. "I've got it! We tune ourselves to Waka-Waka here, and walk right into the Gardens, and then tune ourselves back to Hogboro!"

"That's it!" Alan Mendelsohn said. "I don't know why I couldn't think of it—I'm tired, I guess."

We went into state twenty-six, tuned out of Hogboro and into Waka-Waka, and walked into the Gardens. We had to pick our way along the paths—it was pretty nearly dark, but we found our way to the little lake where we had first made contact with the Waka-Waka plane of existence. We sat down in the same spot and went into state twenty-six. Something was wrong!

"This isn't working," I said.

"I know. Try again," Alan Mendelsohn said.

We weren't quite making contact. We'd get almost all the way into the Hogboro plane, but not quite—there would still be a little contact with Waka-Waka left.

"It's too late," I said. I was starting to get really scared.

"We have to keep trying," Alan Mendelsohn said.

We tried again and again. Each time we nearly made it, but not quite.

"We're stuck," I said.

"We can't be," Alan Mendelsohn said. "We must be doing something wrong. Look! Let's do it once more—but this time don't try—just do it—like the time we made the Omega Meter play 'Jingle Bells'!"

It worked! We got through. We both knew that we

were in Hogboro, one hundred percent. We collapsed on the ground.

"Now we face the problem of getting *out* of Noel Wallaby's junkyard," Alan Mendelsohn said.

"That's right!" I said. "I hadn't thought of that. We might wind up locked up in here for the whole weekend." Somehow, that didn't worry me so much now that we had escaped from Waka-Waka and were securely back in good old Hogboro.

"Of course, the problem is different when viewed from the inside," Alan Mendelsohn said. "When we were out there, we just had our bodies. Inside there are tools, ladders, and everything we need. The only question is, will Fafner be friendly or not?"

It turned out that Fafner was only programmed to act fierce if you approached the junkyard from the street side. He was not very interested in us at all when we approached from the tangle of foliage that marked the edge of what was left (in our plane) of Hergeschleimer's Oriental Gardens. In Noel Wallaby's shack we found a big rusty pair of pliers, and there were lots of old ladders. It was perfectly easy to break out of the junkyard. We didn't cut the barbed wire—just unhooked it at one point, and we used two ladders, one on each side of the fence. When we were over, Alan Mendelsohn repaired the barbed wire, and we sort of slid the second ladder back into the junkyard, so nobody else would be able to break in.

We were both late for supper, and so tired on the way back from Noel Wallaby's junkyard that we didn't say a word to one another.

"Alan, tomorrow I want to ask you a whole bunch of questions," I said.

"OK, tomorrow," he said, as he dropped me off at my house.

44

I never saw Alan Mendelsohn again. It's funny, I had a sort of feeling that I would never see him again when he dropped me off outside my house that night, after we got back from our adventure in the Waka-Waka plane of existence.

When I got home, I thought I was going to drop right into bed—but I got a sort of second wind. I ate my supper, listened to my parents holler at me for staying out too late, and then I felt wide awake. There was nothing in particular I wanted to do—I just sort of ran over the details of my adventure with Alan Mendelsohn and watched television with my family. On Saturday nights I am allowed to stay up late, so I got to watch the late news.

It was some late news! It seems that in the course of the evening *hundreds* and *thousands* of people had called the televison station, the police, the air force, the mayor, the White House, and each other to report UFO sightings. Now these were not your usual lights in the sky—this was a real spaceship! They could see the rivets in the hull, scratches in the metal; they could even see into the windows—they could see guys wearing green sweaters inside, working the controls! Lots of people had snapped pictures of the spaceship, which had hovered over the housetops of Hogboro and West Kangaroo Park for almost an hour. A couple of times the spaceship had seemed to land! The whole news program was about the UFO sighting, with interviews of the mayor, the chief of police, some science-fiction writer who was visiting Hogboro, people who had seen the spaceship—everybody!

My mother was scared. My father thought it was a publicity stunt for some movie. I thought it was real— just a spaceship visiting Hogboro. We had a big discussion about it. In the end, my father convinced my mother—which was good for me, because at one point she had made up her mind not to let me go out of the house anymore. I didn't convince anybody. My father said that if the spaceship were real it would belong to the good old United States, and when the White House was called, the President would have explained the whole thing. He was absolutely sure that the whole thing was just a promotion for some space movie that would be coming to the local theaters in a week or two. It was nice to have a family discussion—even if my parents were completely wrong about everything. We usually didn't have anything to talk about.

In the morning, I wanted to hear what Alan Mendelsohn would have to say about the spaceship—although, as I said, I had this funny feeling that Alan Mendelsohn was gone. It was just a feeling, though—I didn't have any reason to believe it was true.

When I got to Alan Mendelsohn's house, it was obvious that the whole family had gone. The windows of the house were dark, the Sunday paper was lying on the porch, the comic section sort of flapping in the wind. There was a big burned spot in the middle of the front lawn—as though there had been a campfire there the night before—only there were no ashes, just burnt grass.

I had a heavy feeling in my stomach as I stepped onto the porch. I rang the bell, but I knew nobody was going to answer. I could hear the chimes making a hollow sound inside the house. I peeked in the window. The house was completely empty. There wasn't a single piece of furniture, a rug; even the place where the telephone had been was just a bunch of wires coming out of the wall. Alan Mendelsohn and his family were totally, completely, and forever gone!

Pinned next to the front door was a lumpy brown manila envelope. Written across it was my name, *Leonard*. Inside was the brass potato from the moon that Alan Mendelsohn had gotten from William Lloyd Floyd, and a note to me.

Dear Leonard,

I had to leave with my family. We're going back to "The Bronx," if you know what I mean. I'm sorry to leave like this, without giving you any warning, but I had to promise a certain person that I wouldn't tell anybody about this, not even my best friend—and that's you. The certain person—I had to promise not to mention his name, but he's a sort of high commissioner of a certain place—you've seen him.

I'll try to get a note to you sometime, but it isn't easy to get mail from "The Bronx" to this place. In the meantime, please don't forget about your old friend,

Alan Mendelsohn

P.S. The fleegix is much better where I'm going!

So he really was a—no, it could have been just another joke. I mean, if Alan Mendelsohn was really from . . . why didn't he ever tell me? But of course, he had told me—he had told everybody. I just couldn't tell what was true. And I didn't care. All I knew was that my only friend had left and I was miserable.

45

I just dragged myself around all day Sunday. I really missed Alan Mendelsohn. I was mad at him for a while, for leaving and not telling me anything about it. But, really, it wasn't his fault if he promised Rolzup that he wouldn't tell anybody he was going back to Mars—or The Bronx. I couldn't make up my mind if the whole thing about being from Mars was a put-on or not. I hung around the house, watching television and looking at my brass moon-potato.

Another thing which bugged me was that I wanted to ask Alan Mendelsohn a lot of questions about what had happened in Waka-Waka. I wanted to know how he guessed that The Wozzle was really Manny, Moe and Jack. I wanted to ask him what he and Rolzup had talked about—although I now had a pretty good idea of that. They had talked about Alan Mendelsohn and his family getting a ride home to Mars on a UFO—that is, if the Mars story was true. Something else I'd never be able to find out.

Dr. Prince telephoned to tell me that he was back from his trip, and expected to see me in his office the following afternoon. I figured I might as well go—Dr. Prince was sort of a jerk, but at least he was somebody to talk to, and it meant I would get out of school early.

Something funny happened at school the next day. I was sort of depressed at first, and then I got angry. I felt impatient with everybody. I did something I had never done before—I tripped a kid. It wasn't as good as one of

Alan Mendelsohn's trips, but it was pretty good. It had some style.

"Did you trip me?" the kid asked.

"Yes, featherbrain," I said. "Care to make something of it?"

The kid I tripped was a lot bigger than me—but I didn't care. If he wanted to fight, I'd be only too glad. I really felt like getting into a fight. The kid didn't want to fight, though—he just walked away. I was disappointed.

In my social studies class, they were talking about the Crusades. The teacher was talking about how the Crusaders were these real brave romantic types, who were models of morality and all that.

"Except they never took a bath," I heard myself say.

"What's that you said . . . Leonard?" The teacher was sort of surprised to hear my voice. I guess I hadn't said anything in that class before.

"They never washed. They stank. They used to douse themselves with perfume so they could stand being around each other—and they all had fleas," I said. I was really enjoying myself.

"Leonard," the teacher said, "I don't know where you got such a disgusting idea. I know there's nothing about this in our social studies textbook."

"They were dirty and smelly and flea-bitten," I said, "and they pushed people around and stole stuff. I've got a couple of books all about the Crusades at home. I'll bring them in tomorrow and read to everybody about what slobs the Crusaders were."

"I'm sure that won't be necessary, Leonard," the teacher said.

"Oh, it won't be any trouble," I said. "I'll bring the books in tomorrow, for sure." I was out of my seat and pacing up and down in the aisle. The teacher had this horrified expression. She was hoping I wouldn't bring in my books that told about the filthy personal habits of the Crusaders. I was going to, though.

I was starting to feel very light and happy. My next

class was gym. This was the one class I really had been afraid of. Most of the time, Mr. Jerris just ignored me, but at least once a week he'd chew me out. I don't think it was anything personal—there were quite a few kids who didn't like gym, and Mr. Jerris would abuse all of them. Every so often, it was my turn. I was always afraid that each time I went into the gym class, it would be my turn. I always felt sick on my way to gym. This time I didn't.

I wandered in a couple of minutes late. I was late sort of on purpose. I had made a point of taking the longest way possible to the gymnasium.

"Well, well, we're glad to have you with us, fatso," Mr. Jerris said.

I walked up to the front of the class, which was all spread out for calisthenics. "Mr. Jerris," I said, "the next time you call me fatso or tubby or lard-butt, or anything like that, you're going to find yourself meeting with the principal, the PTA, and maybe appearing in a court of law, with that stupid whistle in your mouth. My only regret is that my father, Judge Neeble, will have to disqualify himself, because I'm his son—but I'm sure you'll get a fair trial before a judge who will listen to all the arguments before he convicts you of verbally abusing me, fines you, gets your teaching certificate revoked, and maybe throws you in jail."

Actually, my father has a rag business—but Mr. Jerris didn't know that. "Neeble, come to my office," Mr. Jerris said. He didn't roar it in his usual way. He almost sounded like a regular human being. I followed him to his office.

"Leonard," Mr. Jerris said, when we went in his office, "we've started a corrective gym class. It's for kids there's something wrong with—bad posture, fallen arches, and kids who aren't regular—like you—I mean—no offense, Leonard, but you don't really want to climb ropes, and get into the Marine Corps, and kill your country's enemies, do you?"

I said that it wasn't one of the big goals of my life.

"Well, maybe you'd like me to get you into this corrective gym class, where you can study toe dancing, and grow up to be a little Commie, sissy boy," Mr. Jerris said.

I told him I'd like that just fine, and it would solve the problem of Mr. Jerris having to appear in court to explain why he was insulting, stupid, and ignorant.

He sent me over to the corrective gym class right away. He said he'd take care of the paper work later.

The corrective gym teacher was Mr. Winkle. He told us later that he never wanted to be a gym teacher, but there was a job open, so he took it. The class met in an empty classroom, not a regular gym. Mr. Winkle said he didn't care if we got any exercise or not. He said we could play chess or read comics, if we didn't feel like participating in the class. For kids who didn't know how to play chess, he suggested that those of us who knew could teach the others. He said after everybody knew how to play, he'd give a five-minute chess lesson at the beginning of each period. For the gym part of the class, Mr. Winkle said he would teach us yoga. He had a paperback book called *Yoga Made Simple*. He said he didn't know anything about yoga himself, and he'd be learning right along with us.

Most of the kids decided to give yoga a try. The exercises were easy—most of the beginning ones could be done sitting or lying on the floor. Mr. Winkle's paperback said that by the end of the book, anyone who did the exercises would be really supple and strong. I liked the idea that Mr. Winkle was doing the exercises right along with us. Gym went from being my least favorite part of school to the class I liked best, in ten minutes.

The corrective gym class was made up of all the weird kids—Henry Bagel, and all those kids that everybody who was regular picked on—the ones who had picked on me before Alan Mendelsohn turned up. I was ready to start tripping kids and offering to fight—but everybody was sort of nice to me. It seems that when there weren't any of the regular kids around, the weirdos didn't mind each other's company so much. Also, we knew we were the weirdo gym class—there was no point in pretending anything else.

Even Mr. Winkle looked like he had been a weirdo when he was a kid. I sort of liked him. We all did.

The gym class made me feel kind of good, and for the rest of the day I didn't trip anybody or pick on any teachers. I left school early, with permission, so I could go to my appointment with Dr. Prince.

I had already decided not to bother Dr. Prince with the story of what had happened in Waka-Waka. I just was going to tell him regular everyday stuff. Dr. Prince had a suntan, and he kept jumping and looking around, as though he expected something to be hiding behind his chair. Except for that, he seemed to have recovered nicely from going crazy in the Bermuda Triangle Chili Parlor. I told him how I tripped a kid and talked back to my teachers. He seemed really happy about that. He said I was getting my aggression out in the open. Dr. Prince was a little slow on the uptake, but I guess his heart was in the right place.

When I got home I was still sad about not having a best friend anymore, but I was feeling sort of good about school. I did a lot of extra homework. I was planning to do a lot of talking in class the next day.

46

What was happening was that I was taking over Alan Mendelsohn's old job at Bat Masterson Junior High School. It made me miss him less to do the sort of things he used to do. I drove teachers crazy by bringing up all sorts of weird stuff in classes. In order to get away with it, I had to be sure I was ahead of the class so I wouldn't get shot down on tests. Then I'd have to do a lot of outside reading in order to come up with little-known, but absolutely authentic, facts to throw at the teacher. There's a gentle art to bugging teachers. You have to sort of pace yourself, or you'll spoil it. Sometimes, I'd be quiet for a week or more—this was to lull the teacher into a false sense of security—then I'd spring the results of my latest research, and take over the class for a day or two. By rotating classes, I was able to create an explosion in one class or another once or twice a week.

I started out to develop a tripping program like Alan's, and even spent some time trying to develop a "missile whistle" like his—but I wasn't really able to get into it. Besides, I found that I didn't hate all the kids in school as much as I thought I did. Part of that had to do with the corrective gym class. After the first few days, the kids in the class started to eat lunch together. At first, the other kids called us names, like "the awkward squad," and "the freak show." Then we started practicing our yoga exercises during lunch. Even after only two weeks, most of us could get into some positions that would really hurt you if you were tense or didn't know what you were doing. Some of the regular kids found this out when they tried to imitate what we were doing. One kid sprained his ankle trying to imitate the Dying Chicken posture. You have to know what you're doing or you can really get hurt doing yoga.

I turned out to be the best chess player in the corrective gym class. Anytime we felt tired or not interested, Mr. Winkle would let us knock off the yoga and play chess, provided that we didn't make noise and disturb the other kids. Also, we found out that Mr. Winkle came to school a half hour early and did some jogging around the track. We asked him if we could come and jog with him. He said OK, and after that some of us—whoever felt like it—would show up just about every morning.

A lot of the kids in the corrective gym class were good students. Some of them were in the same classes with me. They liked the Alan Mendelsohn imitation I was doing, and sometimes they would back me up. After a while, some of us started to team up on research projects so we could really confound our teachers.

So the next time grades came out, I discovered I was getting all A's—even in gym! My parents were pleased, and so was Dr. Prince, who took all the credit for everything. My parents wanted to give me a present for straightening out, and getting good grades, and not being crazy anymore. I told them I wanted to throw a party. They said OK, and I wound up taking the whole corrective gym class and Mr. Winkle out for a meal at the Bermuda Triangle Chili Parlor. I hadn't been there since Alan Mendelsohn disappeared. I thought it would depress me too much, but I felt like taking all my friends there. I considered inviting Dr. Prince too, but I remembered the bad experience he'd had there, and decided not to even mention it to him.

So there we were, enjoying our second helpings of Green Death Chili, when who should walk in but Samuel Klugarsh!

"Leonard! My old pupil!" Samuel Klugarsh shouted. "Where have you been all these weeks?"

"I've been meaning to come and see you, Mr. Klugarsh," I said. "I've got a message for the Mad Guru. Will you tell him that his brother, Lance Hergeschleimer, is alive and well, and living in Waka-Waka?"

"We know all about it," Samuel Klugarsh said. "Klugarsh Extraplanar Scientific Associates has been getting a lot of brand-new information of late—but I'm so glad to see you. I've got a message for you too. Clarence Yojimbo was here a few weeks ago and wanted to get in touch with you, but I never did know where you lived. The folk-singing thing in New York didn't work out, you know. Poor fellow—he was very disappointed. Wants to go into the health food business in the fourteenth existential plane of Saturn."

"What did Clarence Yojimbo want to see me about?" I asked.

"He wanted to give you something," Samuel Klugarsh said. "In fact, he left it with me. If you like, I'll just nip around to the shop and get it. Then I'll come back and you can introduce me to your friends, and we'll have three or four bowls of Green Death together."

Samuel Klugarsh rushed out of the Bermuda Triangle Chili Parlor. He was back in two minutes with a strange metallic envelope in his hand. I opened it. Inside was a note on a sheet of something that looked like metal, but felt like plastic. It was from Alan Mendelsohn! It said:

Dear Leonard,

My parents want you to ask your parents if it would be OK for you to spend your summer vacation with me, here in "The Bronx" (if you know what I mean). If they say yes, our friend Rolzup will be able to arrange all the details.

Your friend,
Alan Mendelsohn

ABOUT THE AUTHOR

DANIEL M. PINKWATER has been a printmaker, a sculptor, an art teacher, a part-time dog trainer, but mostly a writer and illustrator of children's books. Among them are *Lizard Music* (an American Library Association Notable Children's Book), *Fat Men from Space*, *The Last Guru* and *Yobgorgle: Mystery Monster of Lake Ontario*. Mr. Pinkwater recently moved from Hoboken, New Jersey to Huntington, Long Island, where he lives with three cats, one malamute and two Icelandic ponies.

MS READ-a-thon—
a simple way
to start youngsters reading.

Boys and girls between 6 and 14 can join the MS READ-a-thon and by reading books, raise money for Multiple Sclerosis research. They get two rewards—the enjoyment of reading, and the great feeling that comes from helping others.

Parents and educators: For complete information call your local MS chapter. Or mail the coupon below.

Kids can help, too!

TEENAGERS FACE LIFE AND LOVE

Choose books filled with fun and adventure, discovery and disenchantment, failure and conquest, triumph and tragedy, life and love.

☐	23370	**EMILY OF NEW MOON** Lucy Maud Montgomery	$3.50
☐	22605	**NOTES FOR ANOTHER LIFE** Sue Ellen Bridgers	$2.25
☐	22742	**ON THE ROPES** Otto Salassi	$1.95
☐	22512	**SUMMER BEGINS** Sandy Asher	$1.95
☐	22540	**THE GIRL WHO WANTED A BOY** Paul Zindel	$2.25
☐	20908	**DADDY LONG LEGS** Jean Webster	$1.95
☐	20910	**IN OUR HOUSE SCOTT IS MY BROTHER** C. S. Adler	$1.95
☐	23618	**HIGH AND OUTSIDE** Linnea A. Due	$2.25
☐	20868	**HAUNTED** Judith St. George	$1.95
☐	20646	**THE LATE GREAT ME** Sandra Scoppettone	$2.25
☐	23447	**HOME BEFORE DARK** Sue Ellen Bridgers	$1.95
☐	13671	**ALL TOGETHER NOW** Sue Ellen Bridgers	$1.95
☐	20871	**THE GIRLS OF HUNTINGTON HOUSE**	$2.25
☐	23680	**CHLORIS AND THE WEIRDOS** Kin Platt	$2.25
☐	23004	**GENTLEHANDS** M. E. Kerr	$2.25
☐	20474	**WHERE THE RED FERN GROWS** Wilson Rawls	$2.50
☐	20170	**CONFESSIONS OF A TEENAGE BABOON** Paul Zindel	$2.25
☐	14687	**SUMMER OF MY GERMAN SOLDIER** Bette Greene	$2.25

Prices and availability subject to change without notice.

Buy them at your bookstore or use this handy coupon for ordering:

SAVE $2.00 ON YOUR NEXT BOOK ORDER!

BANTAM BOOKS 🐓
Shop-at-Home
Catalog

Now you can have a complete, up-to-date catalog of Bantam's inventory of over 1,600 titles—including hard-to-find books. And, you can save $2.00 on your next order by taking advantage of the money-saving coupon you'll find in this illustrated catalog. Choose from fiction and non-fiction titles, including mysteries, historical novels, westerns, cookbooks, romances, biographies, family living, health, and more. You'll find a description of most titles. Arranged by categoreis, the catalog makes it easy to find your favorite books and authors and to discover new ones.

So don't delay—send for this shop-at-home catalog and save money on your next book order.

Just send us your name and address and 50¢ to defray postage and handling costs.